THE PROCTORS!

There was the unmistakable ringing song of transporter materialization that suddenly filled the air of the glade.

A squad of black-helmeted, armored, and armed men, their very tall and lean bodies covered with bulletproof plates and each with a sigil of authority on his shoulder, materialized in strategic locations around the glade.

"Proctors!" Orun warned Kirk, and started to run—and then stopped in his tracks as one of the black-garbed forms fired a handgun twice over his head. . .

And the landing party from the *Enterprise* suddenly found themselves completely surrounded by tall armed men, each with a handgun pointed at them.

Look for other *Star Trek* fiction from
Timescape Books/Pocket Books

THE ABODE OF LIFE

LEE CORREY

A STAR TREK®
NOVEL

A TIMESCAPE BOOK

PUBLISHED BY POCKET BOOKS NEW YORK

Another *Original* publication of TIMESCAPE BOOKS

A Timescape Book published by
POCKET BOOKS, a Simon & Schuster division of
GULF & WESTERN CORPORATION
1230 Avenue of the Americas, New York, N.Y. 10020

ISBN: 0-671-47719-6

First Timescape Books printing May, 1982

10 9 8 7 6 5 4 3 2

**TO
CAROLYN AND LEW**

Chapter One

"May I call to your attention, Captain, that our present course takes us disturbingly near the reported gravitational turbulence reported by Federation ships in this sector of the Orion Arm?" As usual, Spock was both punctilious and logically correct in his assessment of the situation.

Captain James T. Kirk turned in his command seat and glanced at where his Vulcan First Officer was looking at him from the navigation station of the Bridge of the USS *Enterprise*. Kirk smiled. "I am, Mister Spock. May I call to *your* attention the fact that Star Fleet Command sent the *Enterprise* out here to investigate that reported gravitational turbulence?" He looked thoughtful for a moment, then added, "I was told it would be an easy, straightforward scientific exploration mission to make up for the fact that we've seen more than our share of Klingons lately. . . ."

"I was present at the mission briefing, Captain," Spock reminded him.

"Then why the note of caution?" Kirk wanted to know.

"Probably," said Doctor Leonard "Bones" McCoy as he stepped onto the Bridge from the turbolift, "because our Science Officer needs to inject a bit of

7

speculative hazard into a mission that's turned out to be nothing but a boring tour of largely uncharted space. As a respite from continual action, this R&R scientific exploration mission's driving your crew batty, Jim."

"I'll second that," Sulu remarked from the helm. "We've held the same heading now for seven watches. . . ."

Kirk smiled. His people needed the rest and relaxation they termed "boredom." It had been a rough tour out on the edge of the Organian Treaty Zone. Not even a month of shore leave on Starbase 4 had eliminated his own fatigue. And he was certain the rest of the crew was no better off than he.

Kirk had actually looked forward to their current mission: cruising along the inner edge of the Orion Arm, taking data. They were far from Klingons and Romulans. His crew needed the break that a purely scientific measurement and charting mission would involve.

"Be that as it may, steady as she goes, Mister Sulu," Kirk gently told his helmsman. "And don't get too lax. I might become difficult and pull an emergency phaser drill to keep you on your toes."

"The crew would welcome it," McCoy said. "Jim, I know we've had some difficult missions recently, but this crew thrives on such things. Give them a long and uneventful assignment such as this, and they'll go soft on you."

"That I doubt," the Captain of the *Enterprise* said. "Lieutenant Uhura, you don't seem to be bored."

Uhura removed the receiver unit from her ear and smiled at her commanding officer, a definite breach of her usual efficient Bridge behavior. "Actually, Captain, handling routine communications *has* been a welcome change. My division needs to regain its proficiency in handling standard, normal procedures again. And do you realize I haven't had to open a hailing frequency even *once* since we left Starbase Four?"

Kirk chuckled at that, remembering the one time his

comm officer almost broke under stress and complained about incessant and repeated opening of hailing frequencies.

"Quite seriously, Captain," Spock persisted, "we are penetrating totally unexplored space where we are not precisely certain of the shape of space caused by gravitational anomalies. The data returned by the Scout Ship *Phoenix* were quite incomplete because they did not penetrate as closely to the edge of the arm as our course has already taken us."

Kirk sensed that something was bothering Spock. "What seems to be the basis for your concern, Spock? You didn't appear to be disturbed during the mission briefing at Starbase Four. Explain."

"I had insufficient time to thoroughly study the data during that briefing, which was exactly as its name implied: brief. In fact, too brief in relationship to the possible hazards we might face," Spock explained. He turned to the library computer console and called up an image of the galactic sector in which the *Enterprise* was currently operating. Kirk rose from his seat and came over to Spock's side to get a better view of what his Science Officer was trying to explain. He found that McCoy was at his side as well.

Projected on the screen was the known galactic region from Mark 10D to Mark 25D. The computer image of the *Enterprise* was shown skirting the inner edge of the Orion Arm about 10 kiloparsecs from Starbase 4. Spock didn't bother to use the electronic cursor to point to what he was talking about; he merely used one of his long Vulcan fingers. "As we already know from our extensive experience in crossing the void between the Orion Arm and the outer Perseus Arm of the Galaxy, there's usually considerable gravitational turbulence at the edges of galactic spiral arms. This turbulence is analogous to that which one would see when mixing a granular material with a liquid using a circular motion."

"Analogous, but not the same, because analogies

never bear a one-to-one relationship with the real universe," Kirk pointed out.

"True. However, the Federation has charted the zones of maximum gravitational turbulence in the rift void between Starbases One, Ten, and Eleven and the Outpost Colonies at the edge of the Romulan Treaty Zone . . . and traffic consisting of both Star Fleet and commercial vessels carefully avoids these zones. There's no acceptable theory concerning the gravitational turbulence on the edges of galactic arms at this time. However, I suspect that such turbulence is caused by the fact that, unlike stellar motions in the galactic arms themselves, stellar motions at the edge of the galactic arms are almost random in nature. In turn, this would produce interacting gravitational fields which, essentially, distort the fabric of space itself." Spock turned to his Captain and added, "Of course, this verbal description is extremely imprecise because of the semantic illogic of our language. I've not yet been able to formulate a logical mathematical model of this hypothesis, but I'd be happy to show you the mathematical model that I've managed to derive thus far, imprecise as it may be at this time. . . ."

Kirk held up his hand. "Spare me, Spock. When it comes to field tensors and translational dynamic matrices, I struggled through them at the Academy and understand them. But when you can get your hypothesis into such a shape that you can explain it in the imprecise words of language, it means you've got your hooks into it."

"I beg your pardon?" Spock put in, raising one eyebrow.

"I think what the Captain's trying to tell you, Spock, is that words sometimes convey a more meaningful explanation of the real world than mathematics," McCoy said with the usual cynical tone in his voice that arose when he confronted the logical Vulcan on such matters. "A long time ago, I learned that mathematics will tell you only the logical consequences of your initial assumptions . . . and since assumptions are rarely logical, the mathematical results that come from illogical assumptions are garbage."

Spock's other eyebrow went up. "Doctor, I see no reason for you to insult me. I fully realize that you prefer to protect the image of your medical art as an arcane activity not subject to the logic of science, but there are some aspects of the universe quite logically predictable by means of mathematics. . . . Otherwise, we'd be unable to navigate anywhere in space."

"Gentlemen," Kirk broke into what was obviously growing into another basic philosophical confrontation between his Science Officer and his Medical Officer, "shall we confine such discussions to the ward room, please? Spock, what are you really trying to tell me? Speculate if you have to. But specify." It came out as an order.

Spock reacted suitably. "If we continue on our present heading, we have once chance in three hundred sixty-four-point-six-seven of entering a sector of highly warped space caused by this gravitational turbulence. I cannot predict the consequences."

"As I told you, speculate," Kirk snapped.

"Space may be warped or even folded by gravitational turbulence. We probably wouldn't be able to detect such a folding until we'd crossed it, because our sensors aren't optimized for such work. It would've been more logical for Star Fleet Command to send a properly equipped exploration ship out here instead of a heavy cruiser such as the *Enterprise*. However, I realize that one does not argue with Star Fleet Command. Because we couldn't detect such a fold in space, we could end up crossing a 'discontinuity' that might transport this ship over very large distances in unknown directions. And it might be very uncomfortable. I'd venture to predict that it might overstress the structure of the ship. . . ."

"And with no advance warning?" Kirk wanted to know.

"Perhaps some indications. As we grow nearer to the zone of greatest turbulence, we could expect to experience some effects."

"Such as?"

The whole structure of the *Enterprise* suddenly bucked, shuddered, then steadied again. It was enough to throw McCoy to the deck, but both Spock and Kirk managed to grab the console and the bridge rail respectively.

"Such as that, Captain. Only much worse."

Kirk was back at his command seat immediately. "Sections report. Damage?"

Uhura's calm and professional reply came at once over the chatter of intership communications from all departments. "Negative damage, Captain. A few people shaken up."

"Helm and navigation, negative damage," Sulu reported. "Holding course."

McCoy was on his way to the turbolift. "They'll need me in Sick Bay," he muttered, and was gone.

Scotty's voice chimed in over the intercom, "Negative damage in Engineering, Captain. But that was a horrendous jolt! Did we ram something? Or was it a pothole in the road to the stars?"

"I don't know, Scotty!" Kirk shot back. "Stand by. Steady as she goes, everyone." He turned to Spock. "Well, Mister Spock?"

Spock was busy at his library computer console, peering into the hooded viewer. "As I suspected, Captain. A gravitational anomaly due to interstellar turbulence."

"An anomaly strong enough to affect a ship of the size of the *Enterprise* cruising at Warp Factor Four?"

"Affirmative, Captain. And more to come if we follow this course," Spock warned him. "The *Phoenix* data are somewhat out-of-date since the stars and the turbulence vortex centers seem to have shifted since they probed this area several years ago. I'd suggest extreme prudence in proceeding further, Captain. I can't predict what we'll encounter in the way of space strains."

When Kirk had to make a decision, he could make one fast. "Sulu, reduce speed to Warp Factor Two, same course. Mister Spock, sensors at maximum sensitivity and range. We'll continue, since it's our mission to explore these gravitational anomalies and chart them if possible. Other ships will follow in our track because this sector of the Federation's territory has yet to be explored and opened to colonization. Lieutenant Uhura, Yellow Alert, please. And have Mister Spock prepare a data dump for transmission to Starbase Four." What Kirk did not add to this was that the data transmission to Starbase 4 was a hedge against the *Enterprise* running into trouble further along. Under such conditions, the data would at least get back to Star Fleet Command, where it would be available to others.

He punched a control on the arm of his seat. "All hands, this is the Captain," he announced, his voice ringing through the passageways and compartments of the ship. "As you're all aware, we're on a scientific exploration mission that has a good chance of holding surprises such as the one we just encountered. That was only a mild gravitational anomaly, something we were sent out here to chart. There will be others to come. And it's likely to be a bit bouncy. Please secure all frangible materials and fixtures. And be prepared for sudden jolts. We're proceeding at reduced Warp Factor to minimize any future shocks. Carry on."

He punched off the circuit and looked around the Bridge. They *were* a good crew. Each of them was busy at his post, doing what was required with a cool and professional efficiency. "Mister Spock, will you put on the main screen the computer analysis of space strains ahead based on gravitational sensor findings, please? And steady as she goes, Mister Sulu. . . ."

Captain's Log: Stardate 5064.4

What started out as a restful scientific mission has turned into one with some danger associated with it—as I should have suspected. Any time we venture into uncharted sectors of the Galaxy, we must anticipate and be prepared for the unexpected. In this case, we knew the gravitational anomalies were here, and they've been one of the basic reasons why the Federation hasn't established outposts, colonies, or Starbases across the interarm void in the Sagittarius Arm. We haven't encountered any further gravitational anomalies, but we'll proceed with care, approaching the inner edge of the Orion Arm gradually, taking data as we go. In a way, this possible hazard benefits my crew because they were beginning to become bored and restless with routine. Because this new hazard involves the *Enterprise* against the universe rather than against hostile life forms such as Klingons, Romulans, and others that we've encountered in the past, it's indeed a form of "relaxation" for us because it's different and allows us to pit our minds against the forces of nature rather than against the forces of alien life forms. Naturally, this is probably most exciting to Mister Spock, who's been engaged in an almost compulsive display of continuing work with the sensors and the ship's computer, taking and evaluating data with what is for Spock an almost feverish intensity of effort. It's been more than ten watches since he's left his post on the Bridge. Doctor McCoy seems unworried about this continued activity on Spock's part, advising me that Vulcans often show the capability to work for long periods of time without what we would consider to be "rest," especially when the activity involves such logical and cerebral work as Spock is now engrossed in.

There were a few more jolts, none greater than the first that had shaken the *Enterprise*. The crew was almost beginning to get used to them. The first jolt had sent seven crew members to Sick Bay with bruises, cuts, and contusions. The second one caught only two people unprepared. After that, the shocks seemed to become part of the ship's routine, a sudden and unexpected happening that served to keep people on their toes and alert.

Spock was recording and analyzing copious amounts of data. A continuous series of data-dump messages went out over subspace radio to Starbase 4, an activity that kept Uhura busy.

Things had almost settled down to routine again as the *Enterprise* cruised along the inner edge of the Orion Arm. On one side of her, toward the Orion Arm, the sky was full of stars, while on the other there was but a band of wan light from the millions of stars of the Sagittarius Arm across the 800 parsecs of the interarm void.

Then it happened.

Kirk was resting in his quarters when the wall opposite his bunk appeared to shimmer and wave as if it had been made from gelatin. He felt a burst of nausea pass through his body such as he'd once experienced when he'd been through a transporter that was badly out of phase. The next thing he knew, he was flattened to the overhead, then dropped roughly back into his bed with a thump that caused the bunk supports to complain with a groan of stressed material. There were other noises that accompanied this severe overload of the ship's gravitational-field generators, noises from both the ship and the crew that penetrated the bulkheads of his cabin. Groggily, sick to his stomach, and very much shaken, he rolled to the floor and managed to stand up. He slammed his palm down on the wall intercom switch.

"Bridge, this is the Captain. Report!"

The intercom was dead.

Only then did Kirk realize that the emergency lighting was now on. He staggered as the ship's internal field struggled to reestablish itself again. When he got to the door to his cabin, it wouldn't open; he smashed the emergency latch cover and opened it manually.

The ship's corridors were full of moans, cries of pain, and screams of anguish. Kirk shut them out of his mind; he couldn't stop to help any of his crew right then; he had to get to the Bridge. The paramedic crews from McCoy's department would be along soon to take care of the injured. Kirk had the entire ship to worry about.

The turbolifts were not operating, so Kirk resorted to the companionways and gangways. It had been a long time since he'd entered the Bridge through the emergency doors, which he had to operate manually. What he found when he stepped onto the Bridge was disarray.

Sulu was sprawled on the floor beside his post. Uhura was also injured, holding her elbows and trying vainly and valiantly to respond to distress signals and calls coming into her station from all over the ship. Spock had taken over Sulu's post next to a battered Ensign Chekov, who was bleeding from a deep cut across his forehead. Scotty, with his uniform tunic torn, was desperately working at the engineering station.

Kirk knelt next to Sulu momentarily, only long enough to learn that his helmsman was still breathing. Then he snapped to Spock, "Report."

"Extreme gravitational anomaly," Spock managed to get out. "Actually, a 'fold' in the fabric of space, so to speak. There was no way to tell that it was coming, because we have no sensors that can detect such a thing."

"Injuries?"

"We don't know. The ship's fields went down momentarily, actually reversed themselves, then came back. Communications are out in some sectors of the ship," Spock fired back.

"Uhura." Kirk got to her side. "Anything broken? Are you badly hurt?"

"I . . . I hit the ceiling," she mumbled. "When I came back down, I landed on both elbows. I wasn't ready for it . . . or I would've relaxed and rolled with it. . . . I don't know if anything's broken. . . . My arms just hurt terribly. . . ."

Kirk punched a button on her panel. "Sick Bay, this is the Bridge. McCoy?"

"Jim, I'll have a team up there just as quickly as I can," McCoy's harried voice came back. "There're injuries all over the ship." And the circuit was cut from the other end.

Kirk did not react to this curt reply from his medical officer. He knew that McCoy was under terrific pressure at the moment. There'd be a paramedic team to the Bridge as soon as McCoy could get things organized.

Yeoman Rand appeared through the emergency exit of the Bridge. She was disheveled but apparently unhurt. "Yeoman, are you all right?" Kirk wanted to know.

"Yes, sir. I thought I would be needed most here," Janice Rand replied.

"You are indeed. Take over emergency medical aid to Uhura, then Chekov, then Sulu," Kirk ordered. He turned to Scotty, knowing that Janice Rand would handle the Bridge-crew injuries without further attention from him.

"Scotty, engineering status report," Kirk snapped.

The engineer was shaking his head sadly as he took reports coming in from his engineering department. "Minor damage to the ship's structure, Captain. We have life support, impulse power, and *one* warp drive unit functioning. There's considerable damage to the second warp drive unit, the full extent of which I dinna know yet."

"Can we make warp speed?" Kirk wanted to know.

"Aye, but with only one unit, the best I can give ye is Warp Factor Two . . . and that's full-out with the good unit wide open . . . and subject to possible breakdown, since I haven't had the chance to check for possible damage there," the Engineering Officer replied, not looking up from the engineering consoles.

"Mister Chekov, take the helm," Kirk ordered. "All engines stop. Let her drift in space until we find out where we are. Mister Spock, give me a position. *Where are we?*"

Spock moved from the helm and walked back to his library computer console. Kirk joined him, watching his first officer bring systems back on line and check them out. "Captain, the Stellar Inertial Navigation System has completely lost alignment. We still have the galactic time base pulse in operation, and the course record and data banks appear to be secure. I may be able to reconstruct what happened. But as you can see, the course-record data bank indicates a major discontinuity."

"Which means that somehow the *Enterprise* has jumped through normal space," Kirk added.

"Quite correct. As I pointed out earlier, the gravitational anomalies in this area could create what amounts to a fold in the fabric of space," the Vulcan continued. "According to the data here, that is exactly what has happened. We were thrown across such a fold in space, caused by an extremely strong gravitational anomaly, almost like jumping through a black hole or Dirac discontinuity."

"Spare me the theory, Mister Spock. Right now, I need to know where we are," Kirk told his First Officer, his first thoughts being of the ship and its crew. "We can run over the theory later when we know where we are and where we're going."

"I'll put a visual panoramic scan on the main screen," Spock remarked. He then addressed the ship's computer in the verbal command mode, "Computer, scan and analyze the visual, ultraviolet, and X-ray spectra of the stars in the panoramic sensor scan. Match and identify any known star groups and give me a hard copy printout of same. Store the data for possible use in realigning the SINS."

"Working," the computer's vocoder-created female voice replied tonelessly.

Kirk turned to watch the scan on the screen. "Let's have full magnification and image intensification, Mister Spock. It doesn't look like there are any stars out there at all."

And there weren't.

At full intensity, the best the scanners could pick up was the faint band of light emanating from the stars in the galactic plane.

"Reporting," the ship's computer voice said. "No known star groupings are recognized. Further instructions, please."

"Computer, run analyses of selected star groups assuming a ship displacement of several hundred parsecs toward the center of the Galaxy and adjusting stellar parallax accordingly," Spock ordered.

"Working."

"Are we still in the Galaxy, Mister Spock?" Kirk wanted to know.

"Affirmative. I have the Shapley Center identified," Spock remarked, gazing into the hooded viewer of the library computer console. "But there's considerable interstellar dust along the plane of the Galaxy. Therefore, I'm having great difficulty identifying any known star groups. I'll need at least two recognizable stellar reference points in addition to the Shapley Center before we can realign the SINS."

"But *where* in the Galaxy are we?"

"I can't give you a precise answer yet, Captain."

"Speculate, then."

"Very well. We jumped an estimated distance of about three hundred parsecs, and we appear to be in the void between the Orion and Sagittarius Arms. This is totally unknown and unexplored space, Captain. I can't locate a single individual star at this time."

Yeoman Janice Rand stepped up to Kirk and reported, "Sir, I've stopped the bleeding from the cut on Mister Chekov's forehead, and Lieutenant Uhura's arms appear to be only bruised, not broken. I gave her a mild analgesic injection into each forearm. That will ease the pain until Doctor McCoy can make a professional examination. But we'll have to get Mister Sulu to Sick Bay as quickly as we can get a medical team up here."

"How about it, Lieutenant?" Kirk asked gently. "Can you continue to run your post temporarily?"

"Yes, sir. I hurt, but not badly enough to ask to be relieved."

"Good. First, raise Starbase Four and report what's happened. Then get me a summary of internal damage and injury reports."

"Right away, sir." Although Uhura's face showed that she was indeed injured, she stuck to her post, inserted the receiver in her ear, and began to attempt to communicate with Starbase 4.

"Three hundred parsecs," Kirk mused, doing the calculations in his head. "That's a long trip at Warp Factor Two. . . ."

"One hundred twenty-two-point-two-five real-time years, to be precise, Captain," Spock put in.

"And that's just to get out of this void and back into the Orion Arm," James T. Kirk added. "Scotty, we've got to get that warp drive unit repaired and back on line."

"Aye." The Engineering Officer nodded. "We can't crawl across the galaxy with only one unit working. We'll all be old and gray by the time we get back to Starbase Four."

"What will it take to fix the warp drive unit?" Kirk wanted to know.

"I canna tell ye yet," Scotty replied. "My first priority is to make sure that all internal systems are functioning, and we've just about got everything back now. I'll get to work examining the warp drive unit. I'll have an answer for ye shortly."

The doors to the turbolift swished open, and Bones McCoy entered with a team of four paramedics.

"Well, it's about time," Ensign Chekov remarked.

"Half the crew injured, most of the turbolifts out, and you expect ambulance service?" McCoy snapped, obviously under pressure and rushed to a far greater extent than he liked. He looked around. "Who's hurt here?"

"Better get Sulu down to Sick Bay right away," Kirk pointed out. "And Uhura and Chekov both got banged up."

McCoy was at Sulu's side at once, his medical sensor out and checking the Helm Officer. "You're right. He's got internal injuries. How about you, Uhura?"

The Communications Officer was busy at her console, and she didn't hear the doctor's question. McCoy walked over to examine her, and she seemed oblivious of him. Finally, she spoke to Kirk. "Captain, I'm sorry, but I can't raise Starbase Four. In fact, I can't raise *anything* on subspace frequencies, not even the usual data exchange buzz or the ship-to-ship channels. Nothing but Jansky noise and subspace whistles."

"Which means I'd better get busy on that drive unit or we'll be out here in the middle of nowhere forever," Scott remarked, heading for the turbolift. "I'm going down to Engineering, Captain. I'll let you know the status of the other drive unit as quickly as I can." And he was gone.

Kirk looked at his First Officer. "Spock, I hope you can get that SINS unit aligned again. In the meantime, Mister Chekov, put the Shapley Center on our stern and hold a course directly away from it back toward the

Orion Arm. Make Warp Factor One. I don't want to overstrain our remaining warp drive unit."

"Aye, aye, sir."

Captain's Log, supplemental

We are limping back toward home, the Orion Arm of the Galaxy, at Warp Factor One. By random matrix techniques, Spock and the ship's computer have located us approximately three hundred sixty-five parsecs into the interarm void between the Orion and Sagittarius Arms at galactic coordinate Mark twenty-one-point-zero-one and a distance of approximately sixteen hundred parsecs from Starbase Four. This extreme distance, plus the presence of considerable interstellar dust along the galactic plane at the edge of the Orion Arm, explains Lieutenant Uhura's inability to raise Starbase Four on subspace radio. Commander Spock has managed to complete a rough realignment of the SINS, providing us with rudimentary navigational capability. Sensor probes out to the limit of range have located a few Population Two stars scattered through the interarm void, but we're not close enough to any of them to determine whether or not they possess planets. . . . And we're going to have to find a planet or a planetoid to orbit in order for Lieutenant Commander Scott to effect repairs to our second warp drive unit, which is completely inoperable. In fact, its repair will require materials that Scott will have to extract from a material source in order to fabricate parts. Without a second warp drive unit, we're doomed to crawl across the interarm void for perhaps years before we are able to get a distress signal to Federation facilities. On the other hand, the jump interrupted a data-dump transmission to Starbase Four, which means that Star Fleet Command knows the *Enterprise* is in trouble somewhere. We can only hope that a search-and-rescue mission will be dispatched, which is the reason why I've instructed Lieutenant Uhura to broadcast an assistance call on all Federation emergency frequencies. However, since we can't count on getting any help, we must do the best we can to save ourselves, because I will *not* abandon the *Enterprise* even if we happened to discover a habitable planet but were unable to repair our warp drive. We'll get home with our data . . . and I will do everything I can to ensure that it doesn't take forever to do it. . . .

Most of the superficial damage had been repaired, the injured had been treated, but the *Enterprise* continued to limp along at Warp Factor One with all sensors operating at the extreme limits of their ranges. Kirk spent most of his time on the Bridge during the next several watches. He couldn't bring himself to admit the possibility of an extremely long voyage back to the charted and populated Orion Arm. It wasn't his training but his experience that gave him a totally nonlogical gut feeling that something was certain to happen to change the existing situation for the better. He'd been in too many tight spots and through too many emergency situations. Not only did he have to maintain a personal appearance of hope for the morale of his crew, but his own personal makeup wouldn't permit him to do otherwise.

He knew the only thing he could really count on was change.

Sooner or later, something was bound to turn up to alter the present predicament.

And it did.

It was Uhura who spotted it. "Captain," she remarked to him in the middle of the sixth watch since the jump, "I'm picking up something very strange." Her fingers were delicately adjusting controls on her comm console. Anticipating her commander's question, she went on, "It's very weak, but it has all the characteristics of radiation from a transporter system . . . except it's behaving as though it were a side-lobe transmission or even a suppressed carrier side-band . . . and it's continuous, not sporadic and intermittent as it would be if a single transporter were operating on sequential objects. It's as though there were many transporters working almost constantly. . . ."

Kirk had turned his seat to face her console. "There isn't anything we know of in the Galaxy that puts out the characteristic transmission pattern of a transporter, is there, Lieutenant?"

"No, sir. That's a very special scan and phase pattern."

"That's what I thought. It's not natural. Can you get a fix on it?"

"Affirmative, Captain. Shall I patch the data to the logic and integrating unit of the ship's computer as a sensor input?"

"Yes. Mister Chekov, man the library-computer position until Spock gets here," Kirk snapped. "Get us a course line on the source of that transporter radiation. If it's coming from the interarm void, it means somebody lives around here and uses transporters." He slapped the all-call switch on the arm of his seat. "Commander Spock, report to the Bridge on the double."

Chekov, plastiskin covering the gash on his forehead, was working the computer already. "I have a preliminary course line, Captain. The transporter radiation source appears to be coming from Bearing zero-seven, Mark ninety. No range data."

"Lieutenant Kyle," Kirk addressed the helmsman, "turn to Bearing zero-seven, Mark ninety. Put that source on our nose. Maintain Warp Factor One. That transporter-type radiation can be coming only from a nonnatural source, which means an intelligent life form somewhere nearby, which may mean an inhabited planet. And that means Scotty may be able to get our warp drive repaired. Uhura, Yellow Alert until we find out what or who is responsible for that transporter radiation."

Chapter Two

"Lieutenant Uhura, you deserve a commendation," Kirk said as they watched the image of the planet grow on the screen.

"Thank you, Captain, but I didn't discover this planet. I merely noticed the unusual transporter signals coming from it," Uhura pointed out.

"Yes, but you didn't dismiss the data as spurious," Kirk reminded her. "This star shouldn't be here, and should *not* have a single planet orbiting it."

Doctor McCoy, whose hard work over the past few days had patched up most of the crew, merely watched from the side of Kirk's command seat but couldn't refrain from commenting, "The universe is not only stranger than we think; it is stranger than we can possibly imagine."

"I believe," Spock said from the library computer console, "that your statement was made back in the twentieth century, Doctor. . . ."

"Probably," McCoy replied. "In my experience, I've found very few ideas or concepts that're original. Everybody seems to reinvent the square wheel at one time or another."

"Well, regardless of the philosophy, gentlemen,

we've located a highly unusual situation," James Kirk observed. "And it'll likely permit us to save ourselves and get the *Enterprise* back into Federation territory."

"But we *are* in Federation territory, Captain," Sulu said. "The UFP Negotiated Exploration Treaty permits exploration out to 4750 parsecs from Sol, and we're certainly well within that boundary."

"I stand corrected, Mister Sulu. Amend my statement to read 'explored' Federation territory." Kirk was relieved, and both his expression and mood showed it. The planet looming up on the screen looked too good to be true.

It had polar caps, a cloud-rifted atmosphere, abundant oceans, and several continents. It appeared to be Type M, terrestrial in nature, a rocky planet with water and an atmosphere. Spock had diverted his efforts from determining a precise location of the *Enterprise* because their newly discovered planet was becoming extremely interesting as the ship came within range that permitted accurate sensor readings.

"How about it, Mister Spock? Any interesting data to report yet?"

Spock's head was buried in the hood of the library computer console. However, he looked up, jotted a few notes on a pad, and turned to his captain. "My survey is superficial, Captain, but I do have some preliminary data that are rather fascinating. . . ."

"Well, don't keep us in suspense, Spock," McCoy snapped.

Spock ignored the ship's doctor, or at least he gave the impression of so doing, which probably angered McCoy more than if Spock had made some numbing, ultralogical retort. "The mean planetary diameter is nine thousand seven hundred fifty kilometers, and its surface gravity appears to be seven-point-eight-four meters per second squared . . . or about eight-tenths of a standard gee. I'll have better data once we establish standard orbit. My preliminary data indicate the planet's in an orbit point-nine-three-seven-five astronomical units from its primary, with an orbital eccentricity of zero-point-nine-eight. Other data which are highly preliminary include an inclination of the spin axis to the orbital plane of only a bit more than twelve degrees. Length of its solar day is twenty-six hours, twelve minutes, and thirty-four seconds with a probable error of five-point-six-eight percent. I'd estimate the length of its year at three hundred eight days, four hours, and seventeen minutes with a probable error of plus or minus thirty-five minutes."

"Close enough for Federation work," Sulu mumbled to himself.

"Good." Kirk sounded excited. "Any atmospheric data yet?"

"Negative. I anticipate acquiring said data within an hour after achieving standard orbit."

"And what are all those numbers supposed to indicate?" McCoy wanted to know. "Spock, you're certainly capable of presenting an outstanding snow-job—"

"I beg your pardon?"

Kirk glanced at his ship's doctor, well aware of the rivalry between the highly logical and scientific First Officer and the pragmatic, emotional, and also scientific Medical Officer. "Snow doesn't exist on Vulcan," Kirk gently told the doctor. "Actually, the numbers are telling me a great deal, Bones, just as your biosensor numbers reveal the condition of your patient to you in Sick Bay. For example, take the diameter and the surface gravity. The combination of the two tells me that it's a rocky planet, definitely Type M, and the gravity's strong enough to hold atmospheric gases such as oxygen and nitrogen. Its distance from the star and the eccentricity of its orbit tell me that it's probably warm enough for our use. There're polar caps, oceans, and clouds. All of these data combine to tell me that liquid water and atmospheric water vapor exist. The axial tilt—about half that of Earth—also tells me that it doesn't have pronounced seasons, so the polar caps probably don't change size. This also means reasonably mild planetary weather. Do you agree with my speculation, Mister Spock?"

Spock thought a moment. "Your conclusions may be a bit hasty, Captain. In general, I'd agree with you. It appears to be a warm, comfortable planet with abundant water, which probably means luxurious plant growth . . . which in turn means some sort of animal-like life to provide a balanced ecology. Because of the large extent of the oceans which serve as a heat sink, I'd suspect that the general planetary climate is very steady, with no violent weather patterns. However—"

"However," Kirk broke in, "every time we come upon a new planet, we find out how little we really know about planetology."

"Quite true, Captain. There's a disturbing factor that I haven't mentioned."

"And that is?"

"This is a Class G3 star, Captain, which is very much like Sol. However, it appears to possess the characteristics of an irregular variable star."

"You mean it's likely to blow up on us?" McCoy wanted to know.

"No, Doctor," Spock said with great patience. "It means the stellar constant—its output of radiant energy and stellar particles from its thermonuclear processes—is slightly unstable. It varies to an as-yet-unknown degree. I'm not certain at this time whether this star will increase or decrease its output, and I'm unaware of the triggers that cause the change."

"In other words, Bones," Kirk remarked, "this star has the hiccups."

"Well, it certainly couldn't be too unstable too often," McCoy pointed out, indicating the greens and browns of the continents as they appeared on the screen. "It'd burn or freeze everything right off the surface of that place."

"I suspect our landing parties are going to find some rather unusual flora and fauna that have adapted to these stellar changes," Spock pointed out.

Kirk nodded. "I agree. We've certainly made an outstanding discovery here . . . an isolated planet orbiting an irregular variable star in the interarm void. It'll undoubtedly provide the Federation with a good new facility on a trade route that'll eventually develop through the void to the Sagittarius Arm. While Scotty and his engineering gang work on the warp drive, we'll occupy our time with the most complete survey we can make of this place."

"There's another disturbing factor, Captain," Spock remarked.

"Well?"

"The transporter radiation."

Uhura piped in at this point. "The closer we get to the planet, the stronger the transporter radiation becomes. It's almost as though there's a planet-wide network of transporters working almost constantly down there. There's no interruption of the signals. There's none of the phase and scan buildup we'd expect from the irregular transporter use here on the *Enterprise*. It almost reminds me of the nearly constant transporter activity around San Francisco and Star Fleet Headquarters on Earth."

Kirk thought about this for a moment, watching the image of the planet continue to grow on the screen as the *Enterprise* approached it. "Any signs of intelligent life, Spock?"

"Affirmative, sir: the transporter radiation."

"How about cities?"

"We're still too far out, Captain."

"Any communications activity in the electromagnetic or subspace spectra?"

"Negative, Captain," Uhura reported. "I've been sweep-scanning from ten kiloHertz to a hundred giga-Hertz in the electromagnetic spectrum and keeping very close watch on the subspace spectrum. There's nothing, sir. No radiation at all. Just background noise from the star itself. If there's intelligent life down there using transporters, the absence of communication radiation is very unusual."

"Spock, do sensor scans detect any vehicles moving in the planet's atmosphere, or space vehicles operating beyond the atmosphere?"

"Negative, Captain."

"Why," Kirk thought aloud, "is there apparently intelligent life down there advanced enough to have transporter-type technology, but no communications activity and no space travel? What sort of a life form are we going to encounter that could develop on an extremely isolated planet around an irregular variable star located several hundred parsecs from any other star?"

"As I believe the doctor mentioned earlier," Spock observed, "the universe is usually stranger than we can imagine."

"And the crew of the *Enterprise* should've learned that by now, shouldn't we?" Kirk replied, standing up and looking over Sulu's shoulder. "Mister Sulu, please put our defensive screens up in case whoever's on that planet does indeed have some sort of space defense system and decides to take a potshot at us as an unannounced and unwelcomed intruder into their isolation. I'll not risk the ship in that regard. And put your phaser crews on standby alert. Assume standard orbit and secure underway operations. When we get a better picture of what's going on down there, we'll organize a landing party to beam down. In the meantime, Mister Spock, continue your planetary survey activity. We're going to need all the data we can get before we can beam down. There're a lot of questions that I'd like to have answered before we go down there because, above all, we have to keep General Order Number One clearly in mind if we're dealing with an intelligent species that's been this isolated. . . ."

Captain's Log: Stardate 5067.7

The *Enterprise* has been in standard orbit around this planet for four watches. Sensor probes indicate the presence of a wide variety of life forms, but there's no visible transportation activity on the planetary surface below. There're no ships plying the oceans, no aircraft in the atmosphere, and no space-travel activity. Yet we see evidence of farms, villages, and even some cities—although I'd hesitate to call them "cities" as we know them. And there's no communications activity in the electromagnetic or subspace spectra. Something lives on this planet, some species that's advanced enough to develop transporter technology and the energy sources required to power such a system. We haven't spotted the energy sources yet, either, although they might be passive solar types.

Both Lieutenant Commander Scott and Commander Spock believe that any culture possessing transporter technology would be able to assist us in the repair of the warp drive unit. If not, there're obviously mineral resources that Scott could use for raw materials to complete his repairs because he reports that the warp drive unit can't be repaired without fabricating new components . . . and we don't have them aboard. Therefore, we're going to have to utilize the resources of this planet in one manner or another.

However—and I specifically want to go on record in this regard—I'm faced with a dilemma. If there's intelligent life on this planet—as there indeed seems to be, although they're ignoring us in orbit—how are we going to make contact with them and permit Scott to repair our ship without violating the Prime Directive?

On the other hand, we may find a sufficiently advanced culture here that we'll have to establish preliminary diplomatic relations between the Federation and their political organizations.

This dilemma isn't firm. Spock's acquired enough data on the planet at this point to permit us to take an initial landing party down to its surface.

Therefore, I'm beaming down with the initial landing party on the next orbit. This is the only way we can get the answers that we must have.

The landing party convened in the transporter room. Kirk glanced at each of them—Scotty, Bones McCoy, and Yeoman Janice Rand. All had beamed down to alien and possibly dangerous planets before. They were professionals, and they knew what they were doing. Kirk had left Spock with the conn, and he could therefore dismiss the welfare of the *Enterprise* from his mind and concentrate on the job that had to be done: facing the unknown.

Lieutenant Kyle at the transporter controls was apprehensive. Sweat stood out on his forehead as he manipulated the controls. "Captain, I'm having a lot of trouble selecting a suitable rematerialization point for your party down there. The transporter traffic is terrific on the surface."

Scotty stepped over to assist him. "Lad, find a hole, lock on it, and beam us when you get phase lock," he told the young officer. "Since there's absolutely no communicator traffic down there, you should be able to lock on any of our communicators at any time to beam us back up. Keep your data channel to Lieutenant Uhura open."

"Do you see any problem with beaming us back up if necessary, Scotty?" Kirk wanted to know.

The engineer rejoined the landing party. "Negative, Captain. I've trained these people well; they'll be able to cut through to us all right."

"Very well." Kirk looked around at his party. "Let's go."

They took their places on the transporter platform. "Energize," Kirk snapped.

Kyle hesitated, worked some controls.

"Well, mister?" Kirk asked the transporter officer.

"Looking for a suitable break in the traffic down there to get you through, sir. There it is! Energizing."

The landing party materialized in a beautiful garden-like glade with a small pond fed by gurgling water from a brook. Trees arched overhead into a blue and cloudless sky. There were artifacts tastefully placed here and there—benches, seats, tables, and what appeared to be statuary.

Kirk found himself not three meters from a beautiful humanoid woman nearly a head taller than he. She was dressed in a loose-fitting short white tunic belted at her thin waist. Hung over her shoulder on a baldric was a hand weapon that looked like a pistol. Although she was tall and slender almost to the point of being somewhat gangly, the alien woman was otherwise totally humanoid except for her golden bronze skin color.

She looked stunned as Kirk and the landing party materialized in front of her.

"Captain, look out!" Janice Rand cried.

And the landing party discovered that they had a welcoming committee of two others, apparently young males with similar dress and appearance to the woman.

Except that they were positioned on both sides of the landing party with hand weapons drawn and pointed at each other . . . and the landing party.

"Cover!" Kirk yelled quite unnecessarily, because the other three members of the landing party had already reacted according to their training. Along with Kirk, they dropped and rolled, bringing out hand phasers as they did so.

Two nearly simultaneous explosions from the humanoids' handguns shook the glade. There was the solid sound of a projectile hitting one of the trees, followed by the whistling of another projectile ricocheting off some surface to warble off into the distance.

White smoke having the smell of rotten eggs, the characteristic odor of exploded black gunpowder, filled the air. By the time it cleared sufficiently, Kirk and his landing party were on their feet again, phasers out, and crouched in a position ready for action—all except McCoy, who had his tricorder out rather than his hand phaser.

There came a shout in an alien language from the woman, who withdrew her hand weapon very slowly, grasped what appeared to be the metal barrel, and proffered the complex breech and grip end toward Kirk.

The two young men followed suit, except that they merely dropped their weapons to the grass and extended their hands before them, palms upward and touching at the edges.

The actions of the three humanoid aliens were obviously ones of surrender and submission.

One of the young men said something in an unknown language.

"Translators," Kirk ordered, clipping his Universal Translator to the front of his tunic. "Bones, they look humanoid. How about it?"

"No question about it," McCoy replied, studying the tricorder display. "But the preliminary scan doesn't match with any of the other known galactic humanoid species. First guess is that they're as similar to humans as Romulans are to Vulcans."

Kirk reached forward and carefully took the hand weapon offered to him by the humanoid woman while Scotty stooped down to retrieve one of the discharged weapons. Kirk had no time to do more than glance at the weapon he held, but his Academy training and familiarity with hand weapons, both ancient and modern, told him a great deal from that quick glance.

The weapon was a pistol with a short, unrifled barrel

having a bore approximately fifteen millimeters in diameter. It was fired by a percussion hammer, and Kirk could see no means for semiautomatic operation. It was single-shot and breech-loading.

The really strange thing about it was its total lack of any sighting mechanisms—no front blade or pin sight, and no rear notch or peep sights. There was no way to accurately aim the weapon.

"Well, Proctors, aren't you going to take us?" one of the young men said, his words being rendered understandable by Kirk's Translator.

"Orun, I *told* you the Proctors had discovered our link with the Technic," the young woman snapped. "But, no, you and Othol had to get into an affair of honor instead!"

"Othol implied I'd broken faith with the Technic," one of the young men replied angrily. Surprisingly, he was even taller than the woman or the other young man, and he wore a bright green cloth headband rather than the yellow one of the other male to hold back his long black hair. "I had no recourse under the Code but to seek satisfaction . . . which has been carried out."

"Yes, but the cost!" the young woman said. "The Proctors have taken us."

"Hold on," Kirk broke in. "We're not 'Proctors.' We're visitors."

The shorter of the two men, the one called Othol, looked very suspicious at this remark. "Visitors? From where? You don't look like us. You don't dress like others we know. And your equipment is different. You must therefore be a specially bred unit of Proctors." He offered his hands, palms up and wrists together. "So, go ahead and take us, Proctors."

"We are *not* Proctors," Kirk repeated. "We're visitors."

"How can that be possible?" Othol asked.

The young woman broke in at this point. "Othol, they may be right. Do you hear his strange words coming from his mouth, then familiar words coming out of the device on his tunic? Do you see the equipment the woman and the other man have, some sort of unknown sensing device, probing us?"

"But where else could they come from?" Othol wanted to know. "This is the Abode of Life in the Universe. There is no other place, Delin."

"What's the name of this world?" Kirk suddenly asked.

"Mercan," was the sound that came from Delin, the woman.

"The Abode of Life," were the words that came from Kirk's Translator.

"Jim," McCoy put in, "it makes sense. They have no moon, no other planets, only their star, and they can't see any other stars here, even on the darkest night. The concept of the inhabited galaxy isn't part of their thinking. When Spock analyzes this language, I'll bet he finds there're no words for 'star' or 'star flight' or 'astronomy.' And if you haven't got words for it, you don't think about it."

Naturally, McCoy's Translator stuttered and voiced the Federation words relating to astronomy as he spoke them; even the simple Translator had already determined through its programming that these concepts didn't exist in the structure of this new language.

Orun, the tall one, had been listening and now spoke up. "Delin may be right, Othol. Their speaking devices are something I've never seen before, and I'm aware of all of the advanced work of the Technic. And the device has just spoken our words mixed with words that have no meaning. These people can't be from the Abode of Life."

"Not from Mercan? Don't tell me that you believe that new hypothesis of Partan's that Mercan came from the Ribbon of Night and that we didn't originate here?" Othol fired back.

But Delin obviously didn't want to get into a discussion at the moment. She appeared to be worried about something. "You're not Proctors?"

"We're not Proctors," Kirk repeated. "I'm Jim Kirk. This is Janice Rand." The word "yeoman" wouldn't translate. "This is medical expert Doctor McCoy. And this is my Technic, Montgomery Scott. We're visitors. We do indeed come from the Ribbon of Night. We need assistance from your Technic. In return for your assistance, we may be able to offer you valuable information for your Technic." Kirk didn't yet fully understand the social organization they'd stepped into, but he was reasonably certain that the "Technic" was the organization of scientists and engineers, the ones who'd developed and built the transporter system in use on Mercan. These tall, ectomorphic humanoids were a golden find, and it was highly probable that they were not so primitive that they couldn't be brought into the Federation. Their lack of cosmological concepts bothered him, however, because such a thing could serve as a major stumbling block to acceptance by the Federation. In addition, it might mean that Kirk would be violating General Order Number One, the Prime Directive.

In fact, he was well aware that he may have already done so.

"If you're not Proctors," Delin told him, "then you're in great danger from the Guardians. You must come with us at once. We were expecting Proctors and would have left here if Othol and Orun had not been required by the Code to seek redress because of an impolite remark. Come!"

There was the unmistakable ringing song of transporter materialization that suddenly filled the air of the glade.

"Too late!" Othol yelled, grabbing Delin's handgun from Kirk and diving for cover behind a statuelike object.

A squad of black-helmeted, armored, and armed men, their very tall and lean bodies covered with bulletproof plates and each with a sigil of authority on his shoulder, materialized in strategic locations around the glade.

"Proctors!" Orun warned, started to run, and then stopped in his tracks as one of the black-garbed forms fired a handgun twice over his head, obviously with deliberate intent to miss and warn that the next shot might find its target.

And the landing party from the *Enterprise* suddenly found themselves completely surrounded by tall armed men, each with a handgun pointed at them.

Chapter Three

It would have been difficult for anyone to tell which group was the most surprised—the four from the Federation landing party or the ten armed and armored Proctors of Mercan. Both stood there and stared at one another for a split second.

It was Kirk who broke the momentary silence by snapping the order to his people, "Put away your phasers." This remark was immediately rendered in the Mercan language by his Translator, except for the word "phaser," for which there was no Mercan equivalent. Kirk was counting on that, because the landing party slipped their phasers back under their tunics.

At the Academy many years ago, Kirk had been exposed to ancient gunpowder firearms, had worked with them, and knew what kind of physical havoc their projectiles could wreak. Unlike the clean disruptive energy bolt of a phaser at partial power, a firearm's bullet did extensive localized damage as it tore through tissue, with its shock wave literally blasting living flesh apart. He didn't want McCoy to have to cope with such injuries to the landing party at this time and under these conditions.

"Stand. Don't move," came the order from a large

40

Proctor who was armored and medallioned to a greater degree than the others, indicative of the fact that he was probably the leader. But he was obviously as mystified as Delin, Orun, and Othol had been a few minutes earlier when these strangers had materialized in their midst.

"Great Abode!" the Proctor leader muttered in awed tones that he could not disguise. "These Technic people are becoming stranger by the day . . . and obtaining more advanced equipment all the time."

"We're not Technic people." Kirk directed his remark at the Proctor squad leader. "In fact, we're not Mercans. We're visitors."

There was dead silence as the Proctor leader tried to evaluate the situation. It was obvious that he was confused. He'd come expecting only the three young Mercans, not this group of four strangely dressed, short, and highly varied people carrying strange equipment and speaking strange sounds that became words through a small device they carried. Furthermore, they carried no handguns, only strange pouches of equipment that buzzed and hummed and sang as they were pointed at the Proctor squad.

"Who are you?" the Proctor leader asked imperiously. "What part of the Abode are you from?"

Kirk had nothing in his hands. He spread them palms up before him to show that he carried no weapon. "I'm James Kirk, the leader of this group. We're visitors to Mercan." The word "visitors" was rendered by the Translator as "guests/travellers/wanderers/searchers" before it ran out of synonyms searching its newly created self-program of the structure of the Mercan language.

The Proctor leader turned to Orun. "We've come to escort you, Orun, along with your companions Othol and Delin, under the orders of Guardian One Pallar. You three are charged with conduct contrary to the Code because of your open advocacy of the Technic of which you're members. The Guardians can no longer tolerate this disruption of the Code of the Abode. Now, who are these Technic people? Why do they look this way, and why are they dressed in this fashion? Why do they speak a strange tongue?"

"They're not Technic; they're visitors, as they claim," the young Mercan replied. "I'll readily admit that I'm of the Technic, but I also truthfully state to you that these people are not Technic. They materialized here only a short time before you and your squad arrived, Proctor Lenos. . . . And I certainly feel honored to think that we're so important that the Prime Proctor himself would lead the squad to apprehend us."

"Your disrespectful attitude will change with retraining," Proctor Lenos remarked. "Otherwise, I'd demand that you defend yourself here and now. . . . And I'm ordered to bring the three of you to Celerbitan alive, not with bullets in your hearts." He looked around at the four from the *Enterprise,* unsure of exactly what to do. "We'll take the four of you back with us as well. The Guardians will certainly want to see what the Technic has managed to accomplish in total secrecy."

"Translator, stop," Kirk ordered his device quietly, causing it to cease translating his words into the Mercan language. To the three other members of the crew of the *Enterprise* he said, "No resistance. No violence. We'll go with them. Obviously, the Proctors are the police, and we happen to be in the hands of the police chief of these parts."

"Maybe the chief of police can get us to the chief of government, whatever that may be," McCoy suggested.

"That's exactly what I had in mind," Kirk said. "We keep it calm. Scotty, please keep that temper of yours under control; your job is technology assessment."

Proctor Lenos was beginning to fidget, not being able to understand what Kirk was saying. Kirk sensed this and ordered his Translator back into action. "Please excuse me, Proctor Lenos," Kirk said with the most punctilious manners and a slight diplomatic bow. The highly stilted and overly polite language of Mercan made it easier for Kirk to phrase his sentences so the Translator would reply in stilted terms. He didn't like their language with its overly formal structure. But there it was; what could he do but work with it? "I had to give instructions to my people not to offer any objection to accompanying you. We'll be most happy to go with you and meet your Guardians."

This willing cooperation was apparently commonplace to Proctor Lenos. He turned his armored head and looked around. "Orun, where are your companions?"

There was a definite smile on Orun's face. "Why, Proctor Lenos, I suspect they managed to stroll away in the confusion caused by your confrontation with these strange people."

There was obvious frustration in Lenos' voice. "We'll get them. If necessary, we'll monitor all transporter activity until we get them."

"That's a large order, Proctor," Orun reminded him. "What's the current use rate? More than a thousand million individual transports from one place to another daily?"

"We have means," Lenos said darkly. Then to Kirk he said, "I have no warrant to return you to Celerbitan, James Kirk. However, I exercise my authority as Prime Proctor to require your presence at Celerbitan before Guardian One because of your unusual appearance and equipment."

Kirk said nothing. He couldn't. He didn't even know what the rules were. But he knew that he'd find out quickly at Celerbitan, if that was the planetary seat of the political power base . . . and he was now quite aware of the existence of an exceptional power base: the Guardians, who must be the rulers, because there was a police organization, the Proctors, whose job must obviously entail enforcing the dictates of the political leaders.

But he also knew that he might be wrong. On more than a thousand worlds of the Federation, there were many more than a thousand different ways that intelligent beings organized themselves. He couldn't expect to find a situation here, developed in isolation, that would have any similarity to anything he knew.

But these Mercanians were humanoid, and all humanoid species shared a number of things in common, including political power bases sustained by threat of physical force for noncompliance with political and social rules. He didn't think he could be totally wrong on that one.

Strangely, the Proctors didn't search the landing-party members, nor did they attempt to take the tricorders that both Janice Rand and Bones McCoy kept running, sensing, and recording. Kirk guessed this was probably because none of the landing party carried anything that appeared to the Proctors to be weapons.

"Stand by to travel," Proctor Lenos ordered, removing a control unit from his equipment-laden baldric. Scotty's attention was riveted on the control unit as he attempted to fathom its use and construction. Kirk also looked closely at it, while Janice Rand focused the attention of her tricorder on it.

The Prime Proctor rubbed his finger across various portions of the small, palm-sized unit . . . and they were somewhere else.

The first words spoken were McCoy's: "I knew these people weren't civilized. Anybody who'd use a transporter to get around the surface of a planet can't possibly be civilized."

"Quiet, Bones," Kirk snapped. "You're in no position to object."

"I dinna believe it," Scotty breathed. "They must have developed transporter technology at a very high level indeed. The Proctor required no communication with a main transporter crew, and the system delivered us here where there's no transporter. We must have gone through one or more relays en route. . . ."

Scotty was right. They weren't in a transporter room or unit but had materialized in the foyer of a grand edifice. It was a huge hall open on three sides, its roof supported by massive pillars and columns of a completely unique design fabricated of metals with beautiful sheens and textures. The building was perched atop a high hill on an island, because all around was an ocean.

It reminded Kirk of the view from the Acropolis at Athens on Earth.

But this edifice was *not* the Temple of Diana on the Acropolis, nor did it resemble it in any way. These Mercans were not at the same technical level of ancient Greece, because from the building alone Kirk knew they'd mastered advanced technology in several areas —although without closer inspection he couldn't determine the exact degree. Their architecture was an indication of their technology, even though it was totally alien, as could be expected in a civilization that had developed in complete isolation.

Almost as soon as the entire party materialized, Proctor Lenos announced, "I'll notify Guardian One of your presence here. Please make yourselves comfortable, and please don't hesitate to ask my Proctors to bring you anything you may require. I also request that you don't attempt to run away . . . because this squad of Proctors is my personal squad . . . and they don't miss."

And he strode down one of the hallways of the huge building.

Kirk looked at his landing party. They appeared to be as mystified as he at the polite and mannered way they'd been treated by what obviously were the police. It had never happened to him this way before. He switched off his Translator.

"Well, we've certainly discovered ourselves a dandy

little planet." Scotty was the first to speak up. "With the sort of transporter technology they've got, plus what I can see from their buildings, their clothes, and their weapons, they may be our equals in engineering in some areas."

"Do you think it's advanced enough that they could help repair the warp drive, Scotty?" Kirk wanted to know.

"I haven't seen their energy sources. I dinna ken if they have matter-antimatter technology or not. But with transporter technology like theirs, they obviously have the industrial base that'd be useful in helping me rebuild that warp drive . . . even if they don't know what a warp drive is. . . ."

"Captain," Janice Rand put in, "Commander Scott mentioned a lack of technology in communications and transportation systems. If the Mercans have a planet-wide transporter system, why would they need communications *or* a transportation system? They already have *both* in their transporter system. If they want to talk to somebody, they just transport to where that person is. If they need to ship freight or cargo anywhere on the planet, they put it through a transporter. . . ."

"Which means they've got very powerful energy systems," Scotty pointed out.

"That may mean that they've already got matter-antimatter," Kirk observed.

"No, Captain, they could do it with ordinary hydro-gen fusion," Scotty pointed out. "That's why I dinna ken if they've got the energy sources. But they've got energy, all right. No question about that."

"Bones," Kirk said, turning to his ship's doctor, "any data? Are these people really as closely related to humans as they appear to be? If so, how did they get out here in the middle of the Galactic interarm void?"

"One question at a time," McCoy replied. He looked down at his medical tricorder. "I don't know the details of internal structure and physiology yet. And it would be of great help to have blood and tissue samples for analysis back in Sick Bay. I could give you a solid answer under those conditions. But they look like kissin' cousins to us. They appear to have muscular structure, articulation, and sensors similar to ours. They're probably tall and skinny because the gravity here is eight-tenths standard and the climate is generally warm and semitropical over most of the planet."

"How about my second question?" Kirk wanted to know.

"I'm glad you asked that question," McCoy replied slowly. "Are there any other questions? Seriously, I don't know, and I wish I did."

"Maybe we should just ask them where they came from," Janice Rand suggested.

"That's a good idea, Yeoman," Kirk said. He turned on his Translator and walked slowly over to the edge of the building, where he could look out over what was obviously a city spread out below and around the hill. He turned to Orun and asked, "Is this Celerbitan?"

Orun nodded. "It's the headquarters of the Guardians and the Proctors. . . . You're really from some other place, aren't you?"

"What I've told you is true," Kirk replied. "We don't come from Mercan."

"But where *do* you come from, then?"

"Probably the same place your ancestors did. Where did Mercan begin? How did it start? Where did the Mercan people come from?"

"You don't know the story of the Creation of the Abode?" Orun asked incredulously. Then he nodded. "Of course, if you come from somewhere else, you couldn't know."

"Where did you come from?"

"From the Spiral of Life that's duplicated by the spiral of the basic chemistry of life itself," Orun explained, then paused. "Some call it the Ribbon of Night because that's the only time it can be seen in the sky. We, the Technic, believe that the ancient legend may be true because there's some evidence now that the Ribbon of Night or Spiral of Life is made up of a very large number of suns like our own, except that we don't understand why we can't see them as suns like ours. Some of the Technic believe that it's like a light that's seen from many steps away and gets smaller as you take more steps away from it."

It suddenly occurred to Kirk that he was dealing with a completely new phenomenon here. "Steps" and lesser dimensions were all that the Mercans now possessed. They didn't need distance dimensions when a transporter could take them around their planet in a fraction of a second.

A world without distance!

And a universe without astronomy, insofar as the Mercans were concerned.

What other fascinating mysteries did this unusual civilization of humanlike beings hold?

It would be a bonanza for Federation xenosociologists.

And if the Sagittarius Arm was the direction of the future expansion of the Federation in its efforts to colonize and populate those parts of the Galaxy, Mercan would become an important way station on the trade routes between the Arms.

And it could destroy Mercan.

Kirk couldn't help thinking of other cases on ancient Earth where unique cultures developed in isolation had been totally and completely destroyed by newcomers.

He didn't want Mercan to go the route of the Aztecs or the Incas.

He knew that his first task, therefore, was in conflict with his responsibilities as the commanding officer of the *Enterprise*. As the Captain, it was his obligation to arrange for the repairs to his ship. But as the ranking representative of the United Federation of Planets and operating under the dictum of the Prime Directive, he *had* to put aside for the moment his starship-command responsibilities.

He had to unravel the social aspects of this Mercan culture first. Was Mercan ready for the Federation and the changes that relations with the Federation would bring? Or would he have to manage to get the *Enterprise* repaired and somehow leave without disrupting this civilization, leaving the inevitable decision on interaction up to the Federation?

Kirk strolled casually back to his companions and turned off his Translator. "I don't know exactly what we've gotten into here," he told his party. "But we will not—repeat, *not*—violate General Order Number One until we find out more about Mercan."

"I agree with you, Jim," McCoy put in. "I've been watching and listening, too. This place, this culture, these people, are unique. We should disturb them as little as possible until we have more data."

"But I've got a warp drive engine up there that has to be repaired," Scotty complained, "or we're going to stay here for a very long time indeed. And sooner or later these Mercans are going to discover the *Enterprise* orbiting over their heads. How can we help but disturb them then, eh?"

"Scotty, for all we know, the Mercans may have the transporter technology to reach up there to the *Enterprise* and simply transmute it into a signal that won't materialize anywhere . . . ever," Kirk warned.

"Aye, there's that," the engineer admitted.

"Yeoman, how about your input here from the woman's point of view?" Kirk wanted to know.

"Captain, we've probably already disrupted this culture by simply beaming down a landing party," Yeoman Rand replied thoughtfully. "But unless we're very careful, I think it could turn into a situation like a woman trying to raise a feral child . . ."

"Go on," Kirk prompted her when she paused.

"A feral child doesn't have cultural programming,"

Janice Rand explained. "No matter what we do, we've changed things already. And this feral culture could react to us in a way we can't anticipate. In other words, Captain, my woman's intuition tells me that we're in great danger. . . ."

Yeoman Janice Rand was correct.

Chapter Four

Kirk wasn't surprised to see Proctor Lenos return with another tall but older man who stepped up to the landing party and said in a cordial tone, "Welcome to Celerbitan and to the Guardian Villa. I'm Pallar, Guardian One of the Abode."

The punctilious, mannered, diplomatic, and almost stilted words of greeting nearly caught Kirk off guard. Then the reason for it dawned upon him. Even Pallar, the Guardian One of Mercan, carried a visible holstered firearm.

In a culture with a *code duello* such as this one, it's a necessity that a person have the most gracious manners, even to strangers. Boorish actions can't be tolerated in a close society such as the Mercans possessed, a society that was truly planet-wide because of their transporter system.

A Mercan was required to back up his manners with his life.

It put another trump card in Kirk's hand . . . because the entire *Enterprise* landing party was not *visibly* armed.

Or so he thought.

Kirk returned the greeting with equal good manners.

51

"Guardian Pallar, I'm Captain James T. Kirk." He introduced each of the other three members of the landing party, then went on, "Thank you for your kind welcome to Celerbitan. We're very pleased to be here because we've been in great trouble and have come to Celerbitan to request your gracious assistance."

Pallar adjusted the baldric over his shoulder. In common with the other Mercans, except the Proctors, he was dressed rather simply in a tunic belted at the waist, a headband of a bright color and intricate design, and a baldric or bandolier over his left shoulder with a number of pouches attached to it. His firearm hung from this baldric at his right thigh. On a planet such as Mercan, with little axial tilt, large oceans, and no pronounced seasonal change, clothing for warmth wouldn't be required, just as on Vulcan. However, this culture was different because it apparently didn't embrace elaboration and intricate decoration as did the Vulcan culture.

Well, Kirk thought, each culture's different, and that's what makes the universe so interesting.

Pallar's hawklike face betrayed no emotion as he looked carefully at each of the landing party in turn, then came to Orun. "You appear well, Orun. Ah, why is it that when a person becomes responsible-old he often strays from the tenets of the Code of the Abode? Orun, your activities with the Technic and those of the Technic itself are beginning to threaten the peace and tranquillity of the Abode. I asked Proctor Lenos to bring you to Celerbitan under a Proctor warrant issued by the Guardian Justice because I want to speak to you about your activities and those of the Technic."

"Guardian One, I have nothing that I would speak of under any circumstances or conditions," Orun replied with strained gentility.

"We'll see. We're patient. The Sun of the Abode will not always remain this quiet . . . and there's the question of admission to the Keeps . . ." Pallar said calmly.

He turned to Kirk. "In the meantime, Captain Kirk,

I'm told that your group was found with Orun and his companions. You all have strange names, strange appearances, strange clothing, and strange speech. I also see that you go about unarmed. All of you must be Technic constructs or products of Technic development."

"Guardian One, we're not of the Technic," Kirk told him quickly and with sincerity. "I'm permitted under my code of conduct to reveal to you as Guardian One, the unquestioned leader of the Abode, that we don't come from Mercan. We're from another place. We're anxious not to disrupt the way of life here, and I'm certain you're concerned about that possibility. I believe our discussion won't go further than this group until we've both determined that our presence here won't cause problems with the Code of the Abode."

Pallar did not say anything for a moment. This was certainly not the response he had expected from Kirk. "You're not of the Abode?" Pallar said slowly. "If not . . . and if . . ." He stopped.

"I certainly understand why you feel that you're alone in a vast and empty universe. I've seen your night sky," Kirk told the Mercan leader. "There's nothing in that night sky to tell you differently. But do you know that Mercan probably came from what you call the Ribbon of Night? Do you know what makes the Ribbon glow in the sky at night?"

"You're a strange person, Captain Kirk," Pallar observed. "Everyone on the Abode knows that we once came from the Ribbon of Night a long time ago. And the Ribbon of Night's probably composed of vitaliar rocks such as we have on the Abode that glow naturally of their own accord in the dark. The Abode is rich in these rocks that are used in our power systems. Therefore, the Ribbon of Night must be composed of uncountable pieces of such rock ranged all around the sky. It's the place where we originated because there's where the energy and the power existed to create Mercaniad the Sun and Mercan the Abode . . . and all the life that's on the Abode. It's our destiny to maintain this unique thing called life in an endless night of nothing except the dim glow of our heritage."

"Guardian Pallar," Kirk said, taking the plunge, "I told you that the four of us are not from the Abode, and you can see that for yourself. We come in a giant travelling device from the Ribbon of Night, which contains billions upon billions of suns such as Mercaniad and billions of worlds such as the Abode. You can't see these suns as individual lights because of your great distance from them. The Ribbon of Night teems with life on worlds like the Abode. You are not alone."

Pallar said nothing and did not move. But Kirk saw Proctor Lenos stiffen. Orun, on the other hand, became visibly excited, as though he were hearing the confirmation of things he had tentatively started to believe.

"Technic heresy," Lenos growled.

Pallar held up his hand. "Indeed, it sounds like that. Captain Kirk, what you say flies against all logic, reason, and evidence. You speak in the words of the Technic, but with such interesting new interpretations that I, as Guardian One of the Code of the Abode, must learn more about these new Technic beliefs in order to properly refute them. I have no recourse but to believe that you and your three companions are important new developments of the Technic, perhaps the creation of beings that can withstand the Ordeal without requiring the protection of the Keeps. It's obvious to me that the Technic capabilities are not yet perfect, for they've created in you a species of being that is mentally incomplete . . . and therefore I must consider the four of you less than sane by the standards of the Code. I don't insult you deliberately, even though all four of you are not armed . . . which is another interesting Technic warping of the Code. As Guardian One, I therefore require that you not be permitted to utilize the traveler and that you remain on Celerbitan so all the Guardians may meet with you. Please surrender your traveler controls to Proctor Lenos." His hand was on the butt of his sidearm as he said this, because he was well aware of the fact that he might have insulted these four strangers and therefore be required to defend himself, Guardian or not.

But Kirk and his party made no move whatsoever. "We don't carry anything of that sort," the Captain of the *Enterprise* told the Mercan leader, aware of the fact that he'd run up against a barrier he couldn't hope to overcome immediately.

Pallar asked his chief Proctor, "Lenos, do they carry traveler controls?"

"They carry strange devices, but nothing that I recognize as traveler controls."

To Kirk, Pallar spoke apologetically. "I must ask the Proctors to search you physically to ensure you don't have traveler controls that would enable you to leave Celerbitan."

Kirk shrugged and smiled. "We're your guests, Pallar. Why should we want to leave? You're the one we wish to speak with. You're obviously the leader among leaders, and you're the only one who can possibly help us."

Kirk and the three others probably could have taken the Proctor squad in hand-to-hand, but it might have led to potentially irreversible consequences. There was *some* communication now between Kirk and Pallar; Kirk's full intention was to keep that channel of communication open and to expand it. He was curious about the Technic, but whoever the Technic was, they were *not* the supreme political power on the planet. Pallar was . . . or at least represented the group that was.

So he silently signaled his landing party to submit to search without resistance. They were a trained and disciplined landing party. He hardly needed to let them know.

The Proctors, of course, came up with the equipment that each of the landing party had—hand phasers, communicators, McCoy's medical kit, and the tricorders.

Pallar looked at each of them carefully. "Do you recognize any of these Technic devices, Proctor Lenos?"

"Guardian Pallar, I've made it my business to become acquainted with all Technic devices," Lenos told him with some confusion in his voice as he turned each device over in his hands. "I don't recognize any of these. There is *nothing* here that resembles anything I've seen before. And there's no device that remotely resembles a traveler control."

Pallar was obviously in a quandary. Any of the devices might be lethal—either in the hands of these four strange people . . . or if taken from them. Any of these devices might have surveillance or probing characteristics—or might even detonate after a set period of time if taken from them. There was nothing that resembled a Mercan weapon. But he asked anyway, "Captain Kirk, please explain these devices to me."

Kirk indicated the tricorder. "This device has been analyzing and recording the various characteristics of the Abode for our future study so we may get to know you better and thus not disrupt your culture. These"—Kirk indicated the phasers—"are protection for us against things on the Abode that may be dangerous to us. And these"—he pointed to the communicators—"could be considered as a means for us to indicate status to one another."

Kirk had couched his words carefully in positive semantic terminology he hoped would be acceptable to Pallar.

It was. "I see nothing here that could be dangerous to us. But I must give you a careful warning. Should you attempt any violence, the results would certainly require the immediate services of your health expert here. I see no reason to strip you of your sigils of recognition and status . . . and there's certainly nothing here on Celerbitan that we would object to having recorded and analyzed by your devices, for I'm certain that anyone, Technic or not, knows everything there is to know about Celerbitan . . . except for the Mysteries of Mercaniad, which reside only in the minds of the Guardians. Lenos, please see to it that all of them have comfortable quarters : . . including Orun, who shall also be our guest as he tells us about these four new Technic people. But monitor all traveler activity into their quarters; we don't want any Technic people to materialize and try to assist them in any sort of violent escape. . . ." He turned to Orun and put forth his hand. "Orun, please surrender your traveler control to me. The Guardian One has the right to restrict your freedom by Guardian warrant under the Code."

Orun gave the older man a small hand-held device similar to the one Lenos had used to transport all of them to Celerbitan, but he gave it up with obvious reluctance.

Pallar then went on, addressing them all, "It's my intention and my duty to call a conclave of the Guardians on Celerbitan to investigate you and your three companions, James Kirk. We'd planned only to warrant the reeducation of Orun and his compatriots . . . and we'll do that after we've had the opportunity to learn more of you and study what must be done to prevent you and others like yourself from disrupting the Code of the Abode. You'll be given comfortable quarters and permitted the freedom of Celerbitan, since it's not possible to leave this island without using the traveler, whose use is prohibited to all of you. Orun, you may remain with your strange Technic companions."

With that, the Guardian One placed both hands before his long face, then separated them sideways, obviously the Mercan gesture of greeting and/or farewell.

"Whew!" Scotty breathed. "Talk about long-winded . . ."

"Scotty, you're betraying the fact that you're only a

few generations removed from Gaelic savagery," McCoy remarked.

"Doctor, under different circumstances, we might have a little workout in the ship's gym because of that remark. . . ."

"See what I mean?" McCoy said with a smile. "We don't have the Mercan *code duello,* but we have our own code, don't we?"

Kirk flashed them the hand signal to be quiet.

They were led by Lenos and the Proctors to what might best be termed a villa overlooking the wine-dark sea of Mercan not far from the Guardian Villa. There, the Proctors simply left them.

"Strangest jail I've ever seen," McCoy remarked, noting that there were no bars on the windows and no latched and bolted doors.

Kirk was investigating everything he could, and said as he checked doors to see where they led, "What did we expect? There's not a boat or ship on that ocean. There's not an aircraft in the air. There's no way we can leave here. And the Guardians have such ubiquitous power through their Proctors that we'd be cut down in a moment if we tried any violence . . . which isn't to our purposes anyway. We aren't in any danger at the moment, and we're being treated well by our standards as well as by theirs. And we've established a channel of communications with the top man on the planet. We're in better shape than we were a few days ago, when the best we could do was to limp along at Warp Factor Two with the anticipation of several years to get home."

"So, what do we do now?" McCoy wanted to know.

"Wait and gather data," Kirk explained. "Each of you has a specialty plus an individual viewpoint. You'll each come up with different data and with different interpretations of what you see. Together we may be able to come up with some sort of rational answer to what's going on here."

"But I've got a crippled star ship up there in orbit that needs repair," Scotty complained.

"Is there any danger that the *Enterprise* is going to malfunction by orbiting this planet for a few days or weeks, Scotty?"

"No, but we canna go anywhere, and I canna get that warp drive unit repaired if we just sit here."

"Scotty, you've got a whole new technology to decipher," Kirk pointed out to his engineer. "You may not be able to repair that warp drive unit here unless you can unravel the Mercan technology to find out what parts of it can be useful to you. You've got a tremendous job to do," Kirk reminded him.

"Right you are. Thank ye for puttin' things back in perspective, Captain."

Kirk whipped out his communicator and snapped its cover open. *"Enterprise,* this is Kirk."

"Go ahead, Captain," Uhura's voice came back.

"We're under house arrest by the humanoids living on this planet," Kirk reported. "We're all right. We're located on a large island apparently in the middle of one of the oceans in their planetary capital called Celerbitan. Have Mister Spock pinpoint our location from this transmission. Now, stand by for a verbal report as well as a playback of our tricorder data."

For the next several minutes Kirk gave a verbal report into his communicator. Then he used the communicator to transmit a data dump from the tricorders of Janice Rand, McCoy, and Scotty.

Spock's voice came from the communicator after this was completed. "I have all the data in the library computer, Captain, and I shall analyze it along with all additional data you send up. I must say, this is a fascinating discovery."

"Do you mean you're excited, Spock?" Kirk asked.

"Sir, my terms were most precise. And it will be interesting to compare this Mercan culture against those we already know of. . . ."

"Undoubtedly, Mister Spock. But in the meantime, we've got to study and unravel this culture. We've *got* to make repairs here, and what we find out about

Mercan will determine *how* we go about the job," Kirk told his First Officer over the communicator. "We'll feed data to you as often as we can. And please communicate any interesting findings or correlations you come up with."

"Of course, Captain," Spock's voice replied. "In the meantime, I'll also keep watch on this irregular variable star . . . which is far from being stable in any regard. I'm running computer analyses now in hopes I can warn you of any impending increase in its stellar output that might create a hazard to you on the surface or to the *Enterprise* here in standard orbit."

"Very well, Spock. Let me know the moment you have any data on the star . . . which is called Mercaniad, by the way."

"Very good, Captain. I'll tag the computer data with that name and so list it in the stellar catalog."

"That's all for now. Kirk out."

Orun, the young Mercan, had been watching this with fascination. "You are *not* from the Abode," he said, his voice tinged with an emotion that might be termed jubilation . . . although Kirk could find no reason why Orun would be jubilant.

"I told you the truth," Kirk remarked.

Orun was both excited and apparently overjoyed, but yet disturbed. "I have heard the Technic theories, and I have believed them . . . but to find out that they are apparently true gives me a very strange feeling. . . ."

"We know what you mean," McCoy told him gently. "The truth sometimes hurts a great deal. . . ."

"Where do you come from? How did you travel here?" Orun began to ask, his questions almost falling over one another in his anxiety to learn.

Kirk sat down on one of the chairs that had been designed for the longer, lankier Mercan physiology; it wasn't very comfortable for him because the seat was so high that his legs barely touched the floor. "Orun," he told the young Mercan, "we'll tell you and the Guardians everything. *But,* before we can explain to you in words and terms that you'll understand, we have to know something about the Abode and about those of you who live here. We've seen many places like the Abode and we know of many people and many living things from all these places. To explain them to you so that it'll mean something, we must know what you believe, how you think, and how you live your lives. Otherwise, we might tell you things in a way that you simply couldn't understand. So . . . sit down. We have lots of time. Tell us about Mercan . . . the Guardians, the Proctors, the Technic . . . the stories and legends about where you came from and where all this began. Tell us your stories. . . ."

Captain's Log, recorded into a tricorder on Mercan, exact stardate unknown at this moment.

Orun has spent a long time telling us about Mercan. A lot of what he's said amounts to something similar to the fairy tales, legends, and religious stories that we tell our own children. They're fables and parables. But there isn't the wide variety of stories from Mercan that there are on Earth, because there's something totally unique here on Mercan: one single, planet-wide culture with little variety or variation caused by regional differences because the Mercans have had their transporter system now for generations. This has leveled out their planetary culture. . . . It's going to keep xeno-sociologists of the Federation busy for a long time to come . . . *if* our initial contact here doesn't disturb the culture so deeply that it destroys this unique discovery. I keep thinking of two cultures of Earth that were so completely destroyed that practically none of their heritage remains: the Mayas and the Carthaginians. None of us dare make a mistake, because if we do, two possibilities face us. Either we'll never get the cooperation of the Mercans to repair the *Enterprise,* in which case this data will sit here until another Federation starship discovers this world. Or we'll impact this culture so strongly that it'll shatter . . . and I'll have destroyed a people in order to save my command. . . .

Chapter Five

Orun's story was recorded word for word on Janice Rand's tricorder. The transcript was later relayed into the library computer of the *Enterprise*, including the comments, questions, and interjections of Kirk, Janice Rand, Scotty, and McCoy.

Orun began, "We in the Technic now have different interpretations of the original story of the Beginning than that approved by the Guardians because we began to discover new meanings to parts of the old legends. We agree on many parts of these legends, so I'll tell you the original stories we're all told, starting when we're crawling-old, playing-old, and learning-old."

Janice Rand interrupted with, "Is that how you determine your physical ages—by referring to the most obvious actions a person exhibits during certain periods of life?"

"Of course. Is there any other way to do it?" Orun asked her in return.

The yeoman made a quiet aside remark into her tricorder: "Mercans don't count physical age in terms of revolutions of Mercan around Mercaniad. Question: Is this because the irregular variable characteristics of Mercaniad also alter its gravitational constant, thereby changing the length of time required for Mercan to complete an orbit? Or is it because the lack of tilt to the poles reduces the impact of the seasons? Does this mean a lack of time awareness and time concepts? The language contains tenses, but no time references."

Orun continued, "There was a Beginning of Energy in Disorder. From this Disordered Energy, Mercaniad formed from Energy that slowly began to be organized. It swept through the Ribbon of Night, accumulating Energy as it did so and following the evolving Spiral of Life, the vortex or helix motion that is the motion and form of all. During this long journey through the Ribbon of Night, accumulating the energy and matter it would later need to serve as the energy source for the Abode of Life, Mercaniad's energy attracted the additional matter to form the Abode of Life. And once the Abode of Life had formed, Mercaniad's helix path swept away all other matter and energy, leaving only Mercaniad and Mercan to form the basic foundation for the Abode of Life. And Life was created on the Abode, including our forebears. Once everything was available on the Abode of Life, the Great Change took place. Mercaniad and Mercan were thrust from the Ribbon of Night into the void, where we could begin our work as custodians of the Abode of Life. Mercaniad became changeable, challenging us in order to keep our wits sharp. . . ."

"Were there always one people on the Abode?" Kirk asked. "Or were you once divided into many groups?"

"We were divided until the Guardians organized themselves at Meslan on the north straits of Fron Midan, where they formed a group whose early history is much like that of the Technic today," Orun explained. He reached into a pouch of his baldric and brought forth a small cube. He triggered it in some manner that Kirk didn't see, and the cube began to unfold itself into a color relief map that Kirk recognized was the planet itself. Topologically, it was possible to do such a thing, but Kirk didn't understand how. However, it alerted him to the fact that the Mercans may have achieved much of their current technology, including their traveler system, from a basic foundation of topological mathematics.

One of the continents of Mercan was wasp-waisted with an inland sea, Fron Midan, that was closed to the west by a slim peninsula and on the east by a large island forming a northern strait, dominated by a city symbol called Meslan, and on the south by an island-city symbol named Sandar. It was easy for Kirk to see how the Mercans at both Meslan and Sandar could dominate and control seagoing trade into and out of this inland sea which was, for practical purposes, the only one on the planet. Furthermore, Fron Midan straddled the equator.

"The original Guardians discovered two things. The first of these was the secret to the Mystery of Mercaniad."

"What's that?" Kirk wanted to know.

"Mercaniad is changeable to challenge us and to remove from the Abode those who are not intelligent enough to seek deep shelter when it begins to enter a period of increased activity we call the Ordeal. Until the Guardians learned how to predict the coming of the Ordeal of Mercaniad, millions of us were killed during every Ordeal . . . all except those who managed to find deep shelter in the Abode."

"What's the nature of this Ordeal?" Doctor McCoy spoke up. "Is it extreme heat, extreme cold, or some other change? Does it kill everything on the surface of the Abode?"

"It's not simple, as we of the Technic have found out," Orun went on. "The Ordeal strikes down Mercans. It kills us outright very soon after it begins. The Ordeal is only partially heat; there's something else to it that we don't understand yet. But the Technic is working on it."

"Sounds like a combination of increased activity across the entire electromagnetic spectrum," Scotty observed, "all the way from the microwaves up through infrared to the ultraviolet and perhaps to X rays as well."

"Spock will get the answer to that one," McCoy pointed out. "But what does the Ordeal do to the rest of the life on the Abode?"

"Our animals sometimes die, but most of them begin a Long Rest. They stop where they are and enter a state of reduced life force."

"Hibernation caused by elevated temperatures or increased levels of electromagnetic radiation," McCoy muttered. "That's an interesting variation on the hibernation syndrome. . . ."

"But do Mercan people go into a similar Long Rest?" Kirk wondered.

"No," Orun replied. "And we don't know why . . . yet. Some of the Technic have a very tentative hypothesis that we dare not speak of outside the Technic organization. There are some who are beginning to think that the Mercan people came to the Abode *after* life was formed here, perhaps to act as custodians. . . ."

"We keep running into something like this all through this portion of the Galaxy," Kirk remarked. "The basic humanoid group is everywhere, with differences only in minor characteristics. Orun, there may be more truth to your Technic hypothesis than you realize. We've seen it ourselves, and we still haven't pieced together what originally caused the Galaxy to be populated by humanoid forms, all related to one another in various ways. But please go on. And please pardon our interruptions of your tale with these asides and observations."

"It's no offense," the Mercan replied. "I'm learning as much as you are. Some of it's difficult to accept, but . . . I suppose that sooner or later we must all put away our dreams and fantasies of our playing-old lives . . . and perhaps we'll have to do it all our lives from now on."

"You're beginning to understand something all of us have had to learn the hard way," McCoy observed.

"You said that the Guardians discovered the Mystery of Mercaniad," Kirk put in. "How did this give them their Abode-wide political power?"

"At first, they simply chose those they would permit into their original Keep. But they couldn't maintain a secret like that forever because of the other very powerful group from Sandar, here on the island dominating the southern straits into Fron Midan." Orun indicated his map. "The history is long and complex. I can tell you briefly that those original Guardians from Meslan who knew the Mystery of Mercaniad made an agreement with those people from Sandar who become the Proctorate. And together they were able to unify the whole of the Abode because the Guardians developed the traveler many, many generations ago from the knowledge they had uncovered as a result of their studies of the Great Change that flung Mercaniad and the Abode out of the Ribbon of Night."

Scotty was shaking his head. "How did they manage to start from nothing and develop a transporter?"

"Are you so certain that they started from nothing, Mister Scott?" Janice Rand observed.

"What are ye getting at?"

"How much technology has *Homo sapiens* on Earth developed and then forgotten as we've progressed? For example, I can't dress a deerskin to make a coat. And I doubt that you can chip a flint spearpoint. . . ."

"You're right, lass."

"Federation teams can dig into that aspect later," Kirk pointed out. Then he said to Orun, "So the Guardians developed the traveler and made an agreement with those who become the Proctors . . . and together they unified the Abode?"

Orun didn't nod; he simply raised his head quickly in the Mercan manner of signifying agreement. "You understand very well and very quickly."

"We know similar stories on other abodes, Orun," the star-ship captain told him.

"It's a long story and not a very happy one," Orun went on. "There were many who died because they were denied access to the Keeps by the Proctors."

"About these Keeps. . . . What are they and where are they located?" Kirk wanted to know.

"They were built a very long time ago by the Guardians, and they're located deep under the oceans —Sel Anthol, Sel Ethan, and Sel Mican. There are no actual entrances. Only the Guardians and the Proctors know the traveler coordinates so that people can go there during the Ordeal."

"A very neat system of keeping people under control," Scotty remarked.

"Look at it another way," McCoy suggested. "It's their way of maintaining social order. . . ."

"Or the *status quo*," Scotty added.

"Is there much of a difference?" McCoy wanted to know.

"There is," Orun broke in. "I understand what you mean. But you must understand that much of the social order on the Abode is maintained by people themselves through the Code of the Abode, which requires we maintain proper respect for each other as the basis of our very lives. . . ." And he patted his sidearm hanging from its loose holster on his baldric.

"That doesn't make sense to me, Orun," Janice Rand said. "How can you revere, respect, and maintain life when you're permitted and even encouraged to take each other's lives?"

"How do *you* do it in your abode?" Orun wanted to know.

"Well, we have laws and judges and trials and . . ."

Orun patted his sidearm again. "So do we. Our sidearms are used only in personal affairs. However, if I'd managed to kill Othol during the engagement that was in progress when you traveled to us, I would've had to answer to the Proctorate for the correctness of my action, with the possibility of final appeal and review by the Guardians. And the Proctorate also serves to maintain social order where large groups of people are involved. . . ."

"And that's the reason why Lenos was after you as part of the Technic?" Kirk knew this question-and-answer session was giving him only superficial answers . . . but it was telling him enough about the strange culture of the Abode that he could begin to think about options available to him. "Did the Technic split with the Guardians over matters of interpretation of the Code of the Abode, Orun?"

"No, the Technic grew from our everyday work supplying each other with food, water, shelter, health, and the rest of the elements that make up our commerce with one another. That portion of our lives is of no concern to the Guardians or the Proctorate."

"Well, I'll be . . ." McCoy started to say, then brought himself up short. "Free enterprise operating in what seems to be a scientific-religious police regime."

"We've seen stranger arrangements," Yeoman Rand reminded him.

"Which all goes to prove that almost any social system will work . . . except that some seem to work better than others," Kirk observed. "Orun, if the Technic grew from what all of you learned in the marketplace, what *is* the Technic group and *why* are the Guardians apparently upset about it?"

"The Technic didn't concern the Guardians when we started only a few generations ago," Orun told Kirk. "But the Technic has grown. It's now larger than the Guardian organization. But, more important, the accumulating findings of the Technic are leading us to ask questions about the age-old teachings of the Guardians. Pallar fears us because of what we're learning and because we're starting to question some of the accepted portions of the Code of the Abode."

"And what are you learning, Orun? What is the Technic heresy that I've heard both Pallar and Lenos speak about?" Kirk asked.

"We've developed new materials that are different from the metals we dig from the Abode, things that are made from living materials and other things that are made from basic nonliving chemicals. We have entirely new health-maintenance and disease-control materials. And we can do things with life that the Guardians don't understand. We've discovered the laws of genetics and we've delved into cell chemistry. A lot of this came from our efforts to develop better grain and fruit crops for the steppes of Lacan, Canol, Badan, Eronde, and particularly Sinant. We now have food crops that can't be damaged by the Ordeal. And we've discovered that the story about the Spiral of Life is correct: the basic chemicals of life are formed in a double spiral—"

"The DNA and RNA molecules," McCoy put in.

"So we think that the old story of the Beginning is perhaps more correct and actual than allegorical," Orun explained. "We *did* come from the Ribbon of Night, but we don't know why the story also calls it the Spiral of Life. . . . If we came from there, is the Ribbon really only like the glowing vitaliar rocks of Lessan, Partan, and Othan? If we came from there as life already, is there perhaps other life out there in the Ribbon, too? That's our current thinking and some of the questions we have in the Technic."

Kirk thought for a long moment before he finally said, "What do you think about our story, Orun?"

"I believe what you say."

"Does it bother you?"

"No. As far as I am concerned, it doesn't contradict any of our basic beliefs at all . . . and it certainly doesn't conflict with the Code of the Abode. None of you have violated the Code, even though you go about unarmed. . . ."

"We're not unarmed," Kirk admitted. "We carry weapons, but none of you recognized them as weapons . . . so we'll just leave it at that. You have my word that we'll not use our weapons except to protect ourselves. We can also do a lot of other things that you don't know about, but we aren't here on the Abode to change things or to show off our powers. We're here because of an accident to our traveling device very much like the ancient event that threw Mercaniad and Mercan out of the Ribbon of Night. We could travel from Celerbitan and back to our traveling device at any time we wished, but that wouldn't do us any good right now. We need to find out more about you and the Abode because we badly need your help. In return, if it works out properly, we may be able to offer the people of the Abode a great number of very good things by rejoining you with the other life abodes that exist in the Ribbon of Night."

"In other words, Orun, you are *not* alone in the Universe," Dr. McCoy added.

Orun thought about this, too. "I can't speak for the rest of the Technic . . . and certainly not for the Guardians. We'll have to see. Pallar is extremely suspicious of the four of you and sees you as a new threat from the Technic."

"I don't understand why the Guardians fear the Technic and want to hold your group down," Janice Rand said. "You could learn so much from one another."

"The Guardians fear that the Technic will certainly discover the Mystery of Mercaniad if we keep on learning and growing. And once the Technic does that, the Guardians have only the Proctorate left . . . and who knows in which direction the Proctorate will go when that happens?"

"But certainly the Guardians must keep up with the technical progress you're making in the Technic. The Guardians could solve the problem very simply by admitting the Technic into the fold."

"I don't believe that idea has ever occurred to the Guardians. I'm fairly certain that such an idea has *not* been considered by the Technic, because we're afraid the Guardians would try to stop us from learning new things and from trying to find out where we *really* came from," Orun observed with some surprise. "I think it would be very difficult for the Guardians to do that. They appear to be linked too closely with the existing Code of the Abode because they are the Guardians of that. They forecast the Coming of the Ordeal of Mercaniad and they are the final court of appeal in our society."

"In other words, your Guardians have become high priests of a semireligion," McCoy growled.

The Translator had great difficulty interpreting and rendering McCoy's statement in the Mercan language. McCoy's unit stuttered, stammered, and finally went silent without completing the translation. Orun didn't get the meaning of the doctor's statement at all, but the rest of the *Enterprise* landing party did. . . .

Kirk sighed and looked at the others. "Well, it certainly looks like we've stepped right into the middle of a rather delicate social triangle . . . and at just the wrong moment. Pallar's already looking at us as part of the Technic and a threat to his group."

"The Guardians may not be able to help us anyway, Captain," Scotty pointed out. "If they don't involve themselves with the technology of this world, the best they can do is get in our way. I think we're going to have to deal with the Technic if we want help. Certainly no high priest is going to get that damaged warp drive repaired by chanting some arcane words over it. If that could be done, I'd carry some experienced witches as part of my Engineering Department . . . which might not be a bad idea for the future, by the way, because I recall watching witches work in the far-off days of my youth—"

"Don't go mystic on me, Scotty," Kirk snapped, knowing full well that his Engineering Officer wouldn't. The Captain of the *Enterprise* bit his lip and thought for a moment. "We're in rather bad shape if we want to request help from the Technic . . . because the Guardians seem to have us under house arrest. How are we going to get to the Technic under these circumstances?"

Orun smiled, which involved drawing his lips back to expose his white teeth. A Mercan's smile was humanoid, but it was a gross exaggeration of the wide variations of a smile developed on Earth. "We won't have to get to the Technic, James Kirk. They'll come to us. I don't know how, but they will. Delin and Othol were not taken by the Proctors . . . and I'm certain they returned to the Technic with news of your arrival. I fully expect that we'll be rescued right out from under the noses of the Guardians and the Proctorate, because the Technic has a few tricks of their own."

Kirk knew then that his worst fears were being realized. He was being drawn inexorably into the social fabric of this strange, isolated world, whether he wanted to or not. The accidental visit of the *Enterprise* to this lost planet couldn't help but disrupt the social order here, especially when that social order was plunging toward a major change created by the confrontation of two groups in what was a universal syndrome of societal growth: change versus the status quo.

The Mercans on the Abode of Life were maturing out of a social adolescence into an era of logic and reason, following the paths well-documented by other civilizations on other worlds.

Kirk happened to have stumbled into the situation at the most critical moment in time.

And he didn't quite know how he was going to handle it.

Chapter Six

"Mister Spock, what did you think of that last tricorder transmission for the library computer?" Kirk asked his First Officer over the communicator.

"It was quite adequate, Captain. No data dropouts, and the transmission quality was . . ."

Kirk sighed and often wished that his First Officer were not so highly logical that every statement was taken in its literal meaning. "Mister Spock, I was inquiring about your reaction to its contents. . . ."

"My apologies, sir. Federation language is often imprecise and nonlogical. To answer your question, Captain, I suspect that we have indeed found a lost planet," Spock's voice came back. "Everything points to the strong possibility that Mercaniad and its planet were thrust into the interarm void by the same sort of gravitational anomaly that caused our problems with the *Enterprise*. I also suspect that the gravitational strain placed upon Mercaniad by the transition was the cause of its current instability as an irregular variable."

"In short, it shook up that star a bit, too."

"Quite correct, sir."

"Any comments on the humanoid inhabitants?"

"That's Doctor McCoy's department, Captain. But

it's no surprise to find a remnant of the general humanoid life form here—if this star system did come from the Orion Arm, as we suspect—since this life form seems to have been seeded rather randomly throughout this sector of the Galaxy. I would indeed like to beam down and compare it to the culture of Vulcan. . . ."

"In due time, Spock. Our appearance alone has been enough to shake up the Mercans. They're having enough trouble adjusting to us, so I don't want you to beam down just yet. I'm sure you understand . . ." Kirk didn't go any further along that line of thought. He wasn't afraid of insulting Spock by reference to the Vulcan's highly different appearance. Kirk was instead counting on the possibility of using Spock at a later point if it really became necessary to convince the Guardians of the ubiquitous nature of life in the Galaxy. . . .

But he was getting tired of waiting. Several days passed during which nothing happened. Pallar didn't reappear, and they didn't see Lenos again. The quarters afforded them were comfortable and pleasant, although the landing party from the *Enterprise* had some difficulty really becoming comfortable in quarters designed for humanoids more than two meters tall with very long legs.

They were well-fed, although the food was different from that on the *Enterprise*. And it was for this reason that Kirk had brought Doctor McCoy along. The party's intestinal flora was incompatible with the Mercan food, a situation that was commonplace in interstellar exploration and even in intersteller commerce. Bones McCoy was completely prepared to handle this contingency. The landing party found themselves incapacitated by Proxmire's Syndrome for only a few hours.

They were free to wander at will around the city and island of Celerbitan, which was just about the only entertainment available to them. Orun had shown them the Mercan equivalent of books—small cubes like

Orun's map of Mercan that unfolded into sequential sheets of paperlike substance with printing on the sheets in the as-yet-undeciphered Mercan written symbols that looked so much like Arabic script on Earth.

Scotty asked for—and got—Mercan scientific and technical books, then discovered to his disgust that he couldn't read them, much less even understand the drawings, symbols, and schematics which followed a totally different set of conventionalized standards than he was familiar with.

"It's gibberish," the engineer complained. "I never thought I'd come up against a technology I couldn't understand. But I canna even get started with Mercan technology."

"What seems to be the big problem, Scotty?" Kirk wanted to know.

"There is no time base. . . ."

"What?"

"Our basic measurements are distance, mass, and time. The Mercans have no concept of time. They use force, mass, and distance with their 'time' unit derived from the work equation . . . which makes it all very messy to handle."

"Somewhat like the number system in the Russian and French languages on Earth," Kirk observed.

"Eh?"

"Counting in either of those Earth languages is complicated," Kirk pointed out. "But it certainly didn't keep scientists who used those languages from coming up with some outstanding work in mathematics, science, *and* technology. Obviously the Mercans have overcome what appears to be a serious mental problem to us."

"That they have . . . but their transporter technology may turn out to be neglected technology, Captain."

"Oh? What do you mean by that?"

Scotty thought a moment before he tried to explain. "Well, you know the engineer's outlook on any system:

If it's working, let it alone! The traveler system's been working for them in a perfectly satisfactory manner insofar as they're concerned, so they're following the same approach. Why should they try to improve it? It's working. Therefore, their technology in that field has degenerated to the level needed only to repair and maintain the system . . . which is always a considerably lower-level technology than that required to design and build it in the first place."

"Well, do you think the Technic might have some additional information that the Guardians don't have?"

"Undoubtedly . . . but we've yet to get to know the Technic and their level of technical sophistication, Captain. In the meantime, I've got to try to decipher this mess of pottage. . . ."

Kirk shook his head. "Transmit your data up to Spock. He's got the library computer to work with. It shouldn't take him very long to come up with a conversion program."

The four of them, escorted by Orun, walked about the "City" of Celerbitan. There were no transportation vehicles on the streets, and Kirk finally got used to the almost continual ringing of transporter activity as people and goods appeared and disappeared around them. How did they know where to transport to?

That question was answered when Orun's cubical topological map of the Abode turned out to be the Transporter Directory. Orun had only to indicate on the map with his finger the place where he wished to go, and the basic coordinates were displayed, the map folded and unfolded to depict the intended destination in even greater detail on a smaller scale, and the coordinates more refined by continued passes through the Directory.

It was obvious that the Mercans possessed the electronics capability to build sophisticated picocomputers . . . because that's exactly what the Traveler Directory turned out to be.

However, Orun couldn't use the traveler because his control unit had been taken from him.

And this really locked them up in the City of Celerbitan and confined them to the island itself, which was several dozen kilometers in extent in all directions. They were imprisoned as securely as if there had been bars on the windows of their quarters.

No wonder Pallar wasn't concerned over the possibility that they'd get away.

Celerbitan wasn't the Earth equivalent of a medieval city. It was so spread out that it resembled no city Kirk had ever seen. There were no real streets. With the traveler, nobody needed streets. The best term that Kirk could find to describe Celerbitan was "a randomized collection of structures used by people."

It rained every night, but the days remained sunny and warm. It was a typical bland maritime climate with even temperatures and a lack of harsh temperature extremes. Scotty found it unexciting. McCoy said it reminded him of a series of nice summer days on the Georgia coast.

Celerbitan revealed that the Mercan civilization was extremely advanced and at least the equivalent of that of Earth, Vulcan, Ahzdar, or Heimal. The Mercans were in control of most of the forces of nature on their planet, and they were using natural resources and energy for their social needs. They possessed all four of the Kahn Criteria: the extractive industries, the manufacturing industries, the service industries, and the quarternary activities "done for their own sake."

To some extent, the delay of several days that permitted Kirk to look into the culture of Mercan lifted a great weight from his mind.

If the Mercans could psychologically accept the fact that they were *not* the sole abode of life in the universe without causing the entire fabric of their civilization to come apart, Kirk felt certain that Mercan would become part of the Federation in an expeditious manner.

The big question was: Would the Guardians accept the real truth and adjust or adapt to it? And how about the Proctors?

McCoy was also busy. His medical tricorder was almost constantly in use. He complained to Kirk, "With all this data, I really need to have my Sick Bay lab to work with. The raw data is fascinating, but I need my more sophisticated facilities on the ship."

"Why, Bones," Kirk kidded him, "I always thought that you were the practical-country-doctor type who really didn't need all that fancy technology to make a diagnosis."

"When working with humans, that's the case, Jim. But I can't even do a blood-chemistry work-up without the lab. And that's an absolute necessity when dealing with an alien life form. Look." He held up a small vial full of reddish-tan fluid. "I got Orun to permit me to take a blood sample. Here it is: Mercan blood! I need to get back to my lab with it . . . and soon, in case some of these blood components and groups begin to break down."

"Bones, I can't let you transport back to the ship," Kirk told him. "Pallar would want to know where you went . . . and I don't know if he has the ability to throw some sort of a shield around us to prevent us from being transported out of here in a hurry if we had to later on—"

"Captain," Scotty interrupted the discussion, "there's nothing to prevent us from transporting that blood sample back up to the ship. We just take it some place in the City other than our quarters, hide it, have the transporter crew lock on the coordinates when we hide it, and then let them transport it back up to the ship after we've gotten back to our quarters."

"Good idea, Scotty. Pallar may be monitoring transporter activity around our quarters or around us when we're scouting through the city . . . but if Orun's right, he can't monitor *all* the transporter activity all over this planet." He turned back to McCoy. "If we get Orun's blood sample up there, can Doctor M'Benga and Nurse Chapel handle it?"

"Why, sure. M'Benga's a good biochemist, and Nurse Chapel certainly knows that lab inside and out," McCoy replied with a grin.

"Let's go," Kirk snapped.

They found a quiet part of Celerbitan with an open, grassy field. Kirk and McCoy stepped out into the field, and Kirk called on his communicator, *"Enterprise,* this is Kirk. Uhura, get Spock on."

"Right away, sir."

"Spock here, Captain."

"Lock the transporter on the coordinates of this transmission. You will be beaming up a small vial of Mercan blood for lab analysis by M'Benga and Nurse Chapel. We'll leave the vial in this spot once you've locked the transporter on it. But don't transport it for thirty minutes, to give us time to get back to our quarters. Is that clear, Mister Spock?"

"Quite clear, Captain. The transporter room reports it has locked onto your coordinates."

Thirty minutes later, back in their quarters near the Guardian Villa, Kirk heard his communicator bleep. "Kirk here," he snapped into it.

"Captain, this is Spock. The transfer of the blood sample is complete."

"Any problem, Spock?"

"None, sir, except the usual trouble trying to work through the incredible amount of transporter activity on the planet."

"Well, they use their travelers to go everywhere here," Kirk pointed out. "We can only hope that the Guardians weren't monitoring anything being beamed from that park clearing. Have Doctor M'Benga get to work on that blood sample as quickly as possible and get the data to Doctor McCoy when he's finished."

On one trip through Celerbitan, Orun was insistent that the four from the *Enterprise* obtain sidearms.

"You're openly unarmed," the Mercan pointed out. "Do you know what that means?"

"Orun, I told you we're armed," Kirk reminded him. "But what does it mean to go about unarmed here?"

"It means that you think so little of life that you're unwilling to protect even your own. It means that you cannot be offered ordinary courtesies because you're obviously unwilling to back up your own actions with your life if necessary."

There seemed to be a basic paradox, a touch of illogic, or a contradiction in Orun's statement, but Kirk was not about to argue it. He knew that one does not question another's cultural beliefs of that sort. He could and would question the Mercan belief that they were the sole abode of life in the universe because he felt that he could substantiate his argument.

Questioning or arguing the gun-toting convention was another matter.

"Only children less than responsible-old can go about unarmed without being considered as outcasts," Orun went on. "The only reason why you haven't been accosted and made to yield is that I'm with you and that you look and dress differently. This has confused people. But I can't guarantee that it will continue to do so, because we're certain to meet someone who'll discount your appearance and the fact that I, an armed citizen, have stooped so low as to accompany you. . . ."

"We'll arm ourselves," Kirk told him without hesitation. "But how do we do it? What do we trade for the firearms?" The Mercans must have some concept of money because of their planet-wide commerce. Kirk hadn't seen it. And he didn't have any of it.

Orun answered his question by taking them to a firearms shop. The Mercan selected four of the best weapons, complete with metal-cased cartridge ammunition and baldrics. Orun simply signed the chit.

"Who's paying for these?" Kirk still wanted to know.

"The Guardians," Orun told him with a smile. "The

bankers will simply deduct the amount from the Guardians' accounts and add the amount to the accounts of the shopkeeper."

"Don't you exchange symbols of value?"

"Why? The bankers keep the score."

"But suppose the Guardians won't permit the transfer of money for this?"

"Then they'll take it out of my account, and the bankers know my account identification from my traveler control . . . which is in the hands of the Guardians right now."

The Mercans thus revealed to Kirk another aspect of their culture that would ease their way into membership in the Federation. The Mercans not only had the concept of money, but of credit or money that exists in the future. Furthermore, they had computers capable of keeping track, and therefore needed no "hard money" such as gold. Some computer technology would, of course, be a technical fallout of the traveler system . . . or a precedent of it.

Although McCoy normally carried a hand phaser on a landing party such as this, the doctor objected to wearing the firearm. "Jim, I'm a healer, not a killer. I'm probably going to end up taking some of these steel projectiles out of one of you before all this is over, anyway, and I don't think a medical man should go around with a deadly weapon in view."

"Were any of your ancestors medical men, Bones?" Kirk asked.

"Of course. Even back before the American Civil War, a lot of the Georgia McCoys were doctors. My family has a proud history of healers in our family tree, suh."

"Then I would suspect," Kirk went on gently, "that many of your honored ancestors not only carried swords in antebellum days, but also carried pistols when that was part of the accouterments of a Southern gentleman. . . . Bones, you can keep it unloaded if you want, but you should wear it, because I don't want you to be treated as an untouchable in this civilization. When in Rome . . ."

McCoy sighed in resignation and slung the baldric over his shoulder. "I know. When in Rome, the thing to do is to shoot Roman candles. . . ."

Janice Rand offered no objection to carrying the heavy weapon. She'd seen what Kirk had seen, and she knew the meaning of the weapon in this culture. "I may never shoot it, Captain. I prefer to use my hand phaser if it becomes necessary to protect myself."

Kirk knew she would, and that she wouldn't hesitate to use either the Mercan sidearm or her hand phaser if it became necessary. Having had Yeoman Janice Rand along on several landing parties on some very nasty planets, Kirk knew she was perfectly capable of shooting first—and very accurately—and questioning later if the occasion should require.

As Kirk had noticed shortly after beaming down and getting his first look at a Mercan "social-purpose weapon," it was fairly crude by the standards of gunpowder firearms. It had a barrel of good steel about thirty centimeters long with a bore of about fifteen centimeters. The barrel was smooth-bored, not rifled. The bullet was short for its caliber, made of steel, and round-nosed—not a very accurate projectile for use in an unrifled firearm, because it would have a tendency to tumble in flight at any range beyond a few dozen meters. The cartridge case was steel, untapered, and had what appeared to be a center-fired primer. The propellant was plain, well-made black powder of a grade Scotty called "FFFFg." The weapon was single-shot, with a simple push-turn-lock bolt. It was not well-balanced in Kirk's hand. Furthermore, there were no sights on it.

The Mercan social-purpose weapon was inaccurate, difficult to use, and deadly *only* if the bullet happened to hit a vital organ. This was borne out when Orun took them to a practice range. At ten paces—about ten meters—accepted by the Mercans as the standard distance where one squared off against an opponent, only Kirk could hit the silhouette target the size of a Mercan. McCoy passed up the opportunity for target practice, saying that he wouldn't be using the weapon under any circumstances. Besides, he found himself busy attending to the sore wrist of Janice Rand caused by the tremendous recoil of the hand weapon.

"It makes a lot of noise and leaves a big cloud of stinkin' smoke smellin' of hydrogen sulfide, but ye can't hit a thing with it. It wasn't really designed to be lethal. Either Sulu or I could make a better firearm than this in the ship's machine shop . . . or we could modify this one so that it'd be accurate with a muzzle velocity that'd really hit hard," Scotty observed. "However, it does one thing very well indeed: it gives ye the satisfaction of having complied with the rules . . . loudly and vigorously."

"Which means we'd better not give these people hand phasers until they give up dueling," McCoy observed, "or there'll be wholesale slaughter on this planet."

They had visitors waiting for them when they returned to their quarters below the Guardian Villa. Pallar was there with six other Guardians, three of whom were Mercan women.

"Good day, James Kirk . . . Janice Rand . . . Leonard McCoy . . . Montgomery Scott . . . Orun ar Partan," Pallar greeted them as they entered their villa.

"Good day, Pallar." Kirk returned the greeting as graciously and politely as Pallar. "We were not aware that you were to visit us. I'm sorry that we weren't here. I hope you haven't waited long."

"Not at all. No offense, James Kirk," Pallar replied. The long-winded mannerisms of Mercan bothered Kirk, but he remembered that he was now armed with a Mercan sidearm, a fact that was not lost upon Pallar.

"Ah, I see that you are again armed. . . ."

"No, Pallar, we're armed with your weapons for the

first time, because we didn't wish to violate one of the basic customs of Mercan," Kirk explained. "We haven't met your colleagues, Pallar."

The Guardian One rectified this immediately, introducing each as a Guardian of varying rank—Tombah, Noal, and Johon were the men; the women were introduced as Aldys, Parna, and Jona. Pallar did not elaborate on their rank or their individual interest or specialty. However, Kirk did note that none of them were introduced by any name other than what appeared to be their Mercan given name, in contrast to Orun, who bore the lineage name of "ar Partan." Someday, Kirk thought, he'd get all the customs sorted out. However, he wasn't even certain of all the customs of a well-known place such as Vulcan yet. The xeno-sociologists were certainly going to have a field day on Mercan, if the Guardians would permit it.

"And to what do we owe this visit?" Kirk wanted to know.

"My colleagues here are experts and specialists in both the operations of the Technic and in the history and interpretation of the Code of the Abode, particularly as it relates to our legends of the Beginning," Pallar explained. "We wish to question you about your origin and the Technic procedures that produced you."

"Guardian Pallar," Orun spoke up, "I'm a member of the Technic and proud of it. I tell you in all truth that these four are *not* of the Technic, nor did the Technic produce them through bio-engineering."

"That's quite impossible!" Guardian Johon snapped. "They're obviously not normal Mercans. Look at them! They're short. They're more heavily built. They don't have our skin color. And they're dressed in clothing that's different from anything worn anywhere on the Abode. If they're not the result of Technic work, where else could they have come from?"

"Guardian Johon," Kirk snapped, his hand going to the butt of the Mercan pistol he now wore at his right side. The Guardian who had spoken so sharply reacted in a like manner. "Your Code requires that a person be ready to back up his manners with his life; we are now prepared to do so if necessary. Your Code, if I understand it correctly, also requires that a person speak the truth as he knows it. I'll tell you the truth as the four of us know it. If you'll accept it as the truth after you hear it, even though it may strike at the very roots of your basic beliefs, we can then proceed to discuss what we can do so that the facts we present to you may have the least impact upon your way of life. Will you listen?"

"We'll listen, Technic," said the woman Guardian Parna. "However, be aware of the fact that we believe the Technic capable of manipulating minds as well as physical bodies."

"We're capable of doing neither," Orun put in. "What we're able to do with animals is one thing. With people, our technology isn't to that point yet . . . and probably won't get there. . . ."

"These four mutants tell us otherwise," Guardian Noal growled.

Kirk faced him as well. "Will you listen, Guardian?"

"Reluctantly, James Kirk."

The star-ship captain turned to their leader, Guardian One Pallar. "Your Code speaks of manners and polite treatment of people, Pallar. The actions of your Guardians seem to be otherwise. We haven't threatened you, even though we're capable of controlling power far beyond anything I've yet seen on the Abode. We wish to cooperate, yet we're answered with insults. We have no desire to unduly disturb the life of Mercan, and we offer to assist you in reducing the effects of our visit here. I have no interest in seeing either the Guardians or the Technic prevail in the struggle that seems to be growing between your two groups. I don't expect you to change your beliefs at once, but I'd like the opportunity to tell you who we are, where we came from, and why we're here on the Abode. Under those

conditions, will you instruct your colleagues to with-
hold their comments and attempt to maintain open
minds?"

"Tell us your tale, James Kirk. My revered colleagues, I entreat you to listen so that we may discuss it
later."

Chapter Seven

It was probably one of the most difficult tasks ever faced by Captain James T. Kirk of the USS *Enterprise*. He'd encountered more advanced races, such as the Organians, as well as primitive humanoid races, like those on Neural. He'd dealt with Klingons, Romulans, and other alien creatures, such as the Horta. But never before had he encountered an advanced, sophisticated humanoid culture like that of Mercan, isolated from the rest of the Galaxy since beyond the memory of any inhabitant and relying only on legends that had probably been garbled far beyond their original meanings by telling and retelling over the ages. Insofar as there was time at Star Fleet Academy, he'd been exposed to many aspects of xeno-sociology and diplomacy, even to the extent of running simulations of hypothetical incidents.

There were going to have to be some changes made in the Academy curriculum in this regard, Kirk thought. He knew he was literally facing the Mercan equivalent of the Holy Inquisition here . . . and it had been a long time since Earth humans had had to undergo such an ordeal. As he recalled, it took 346 years for religious leaders on Earth to pardon and forgive Galileo. Kirk hoped that it wouldn't take that long on Mercan.

Kirk began by asking, "Your legends of the Beginning say that Mercaniad and the Abode came from the Ribbon of Night, sometimes called the Spiral of Life, correct?"

Pallar nodded. "Our remote ancestors came from the Ribbon of Night once the Abode was completely equipped to serve as the Abode of Life in the Universe . . . and it's been our duty to maintain the Abode of Life as the sole place where life exists in the Universe. . . ."

"But all this started in the Ribbon, right?" Kirk persisted.

"Unquestionably," Tombah interjected. "I've made a study of the ancient legends from the remnants of the records that are still in our sacred possession here. There's no question of the fact that Mercaniad and the Abode, with everything on the Abode as you see it today, once came from the Ribbon of Night."

"And, Guardian Tombah, since you're a recognized expert on the subject, how were Mercaniad and the Abode formed in the Ribbon?" Kirk persisted, trying the approach of asking questions in such a way that the answers of the Guardians would eventually lead them to the final conclusions Kirk desired—an old trick of debate that he'd learned the hard way from Lieutenant Commander John Woods, one of the most irascible and brilliant of his professors at the Academy those long years ago.

"By accretion of the glowing rocks of vitaliar material of which the Ribbon is composed," the Guardian replied without pause. "Much of the Abode is made up of this vitaliar material. The same phenomenon that causes vitaliar to glow with light in the dark provided the energy to assemble the basic building blocks of life, the spiral molecules that contain the genetic code. . . ."

"Have you been able to duplicate this process?" Kirk wanted to know.

"Of course not. We are here to ensure that life survives, not to attempt to duplicate it other than by natural processes," Tombah snapped back.

"The Technic has done so," Orun put in. "It is no secret that we can now reproduce the spiral molecule from basic chemicals. However, we cannot yet assemble such molecules to produce a living organism as simple as a mud-worm."

"Why, *that* is a gross violation of the Code of the Abode!" It was the first time that the woman Aldys had spoken up, and it was with high indignation.

"We are creating life, not destroying it," Orun pointed out.

Pallar raised his hand. "Honored colleagues and guests. We, the Guardians, came here today to ask questions and get answers. Instead, we have been answering questions. And we have been telling these Technic people things that every Mercan knows from the time of learning-old. James Kirk, you're intelligent and clever. But *we* will ask the questions."

"Honored Guardian," Kirk fired back, "you gave us permission to tell our story of where we came from. You didn't stipulate *how* we were to tell that story. I choose to do so by an ancient technique known to us as the Socratic Method. When I finish, you'll know where we come from and why. May I proceed?"

"You speak of methods we know not of," Aldys replied.

"In that case, perhaps you'll learn as much from us as we're learning from you, leading to a closer friendship because of shared information," Kirk said smoothly. "I'm certain that Guardians don't stop learning things once they have attained the status of Guardianship."

"Proceed, James Kirk. Whether your story is true or not, I must state a fascination for your logical thinking processes," Pallar admitted.

"I wish Spock had heard that," McCoy muttered to himself.

"Very well, Guardians of the Code of the Abode, the four of us look different and speak differently because we came from the same place that *you* came from: the Ribbon of Night, which is truly the Spiral of Life because it contains billions of stars like Mercaniad and places like the Abode." Kirk held up his hand to quell the explosion of emotional comments that started to come from all the Guardians at this remark. "This information doesn't invalidate the Code of the Abode. The Abode is indeed the *only* place where life exists in this part of the Universe. But life *does* exist elsewhere in the Ribbon of Night where your ancestors came from. Some of this life is similar to you—as you can see. We all come from an abode called Earth or Sol III. There are several hundred more of us who together have come to the Abode by accident from the Ribbon of Light in the same manner that Mercaniad and the Abode were transported here. Our traveling world that we built ourselves is in your sky now, and we can make it visible to you tonight as it passes overhead. We're prepared to prove to you, Guardians, the truth of every word I've said. Doctor Leonard McCoy is prepared to work with your Guardian medical and health experts to show you that we're similar to you and yet different. . . ."

"This is gross nonsense!" Johon snorted. "Guardian Pallar, must we listen to such obvious fabrications of untruths that fly in the face of the Code of the Abode and all our legends and truths of the Beginning?"

"There is nothing incompatible between your beliefs and what I've told you," Kirk put in quickly. "It is perhaps an extension of your beliefs—additional information, if you will. But we have no intention of attempting to undermine your authority on the Abode or to destroy your cultural heritage because that is contrary to *our* basic code of behavior."

"The Technic manipulation of their bodies and minds has rendered them all quite insane, Guardian Pallar," Noal broke in. "I submit that it's quite proper for us to detain them as animals and to undertake a thorough biological examination of them in order to assess this latest Technic development. Since there are four of them, this provides us with sufficient samples to perform autopsies on one or two of them while at the same time leaving live ones for psychological probing. . . ."

"Over my dead body!" Scotty growled.

"Shut up, Scotty. That's the way it may be," Kirk told him quietly.

"It's gettin' a bit out-o'-hand, Captain. Time we showed them what we can do."

"No, Scotty, they'll just consider it to be another Technic development that they didn't know about," McCoy observed.

"Don't worry, they're not going to use us as guinea pigs," Kirk promised. But he knew he was going to have to think fast to work his way out of this one. If he couldn't work with the Guardians as the political-social leaders of this planet, he'd have to work with the unknown Technic, whose only contact with them at this point was their fellow prisoner, Orun.

But why hadn't the Technic shown up to rescue Orun?

Pallar was still considering the remark from Guardian Noal. "That would take a full conclave of the Guardians. Permission to do such things to a life form that so closely resembles us would be a matter of utmost concern and would require considerable discussion. I cannot order what you suggest, Guardian Noal."

"Then I request that messengers be sent to convene the Guardian Group," Noal replied.

The Guardian woman Parna held up both hands and spoke for the first time. "Guardian One, it will be difficult to comply with Guardian Noal's request. Observations of Mercaniad indicate that a major Ordeal will occur before we'll be able to convene. Our efforts will have to be diverted to the Protection of Life against the Ordeal. We must begin moving people into the Keeps before Mercaniad dips below the horizon at Celerbitan tomorrow."

"Duty before all else," Pallar sighed.

"I therefore suggest that these Technic constructs be detained in the Guardian Keep until the Ordeal is finished. Then we may proceed with our conclave and studies," Guardian Jona suggested.

"I have a better idea," Guardian Noal put in. "As the Guardian expert on health and medicine, I submit to you that these constructs may have been designed by the Technic to withstand the Ordeal. I think we should leave two of them on the surface to find out if this is true and take two of them into our Keep for later study. If two of them survive on the surface, we'll still have four to work with. If they don't, we'll have two of them that have been protected in our Keep."

Kirk felt that it was time to assert himself as a Mercan if that was how the Guardians were going to treat him. "Guardian Noal," Kirk growled, slowly and deliberately moving his hand toward the butt of the pistol hung from the baldric at his right side. "The four of us take offense at being labeled animals. We demand an immediate apology or satisfaction. All *four* of us demand this!" He noted with pleasure that Scotty took the hint and had moved his hand to his gun, followed by Janice Rand and Bones McCoy.

Pallar quickly stepped between Kirk and Noal. "Guardian Noal! You will refrain from such comments! Even if these four are Technic constructs, they are still Mercan and are behaving according to the Code of the Abode . . . regardless of their beliefs. They are much too valuable to be allowed to engage in a duel with you or anyone else. Should you prevail over *any* of them, I would be forced to declare that you had destroyed a valuable individual and that you had provoked the engagement. Unhand your weapons, all of you!"

"I don't understand your classification of them as

valuable, Guardian One," Noal said, removing his hand from his gun.

There was a sly look on Pallar's long face. "Consider it in this light, fellow Guardians: they are Technic people. As Guardians, we have the age-old right to deny traveling to the Keeps during the Ordeal. We will therefore deny them this right . . . and deny Orun as well. The consequences will certainly fall in our favor. . . ."

"Of course." Guardian Johan brightened. "If we make this known—and it will be the first time in many Ordeals that persons were denied the safety of the Keeps—the Technic is certain to attempt to rescue them."

"At which point we'll be able to secure additional Technic people for questioning, perhaps some whom we do not know of at this time," Guardian Jona added.

"And if they're not rescued by the Technic, we'll find out whether or not these Technic constructs can withstand the Ordeal outside the Keeps," Guardian Noal said with head held high in approval. "However, may I suggest that we deny the Keeps to only two of them, Guardian One? If they don't survive, we'll still have two."

"Who do you suggest should be denied?" Pallar asked.

"James Kirk, who's voiced these heretical statements, and the obvious Technic member of the group, Engineer Montgomery Scott," Tombah recommended.

"Very well," Pallar said in obvious conclusion, and drew himself up to his imposing full height. "It is the ruling of the Guardian Leaders One through Seven that James Kirk, Montgomery Scott, and Orun ar Pathan be denied the protection of the Keeps during the forthcoming Ordeal because of their refusal to fully accept the tenets of the Code of the Abode and their belief in the heresies of the Technic. So be it!" He spread his hands before the five literal prisoners, mannered as usual in the Mercan tradition, and added, "We must now unfortunately take our leave. Proctor Lenos and his squad will arrive for McCoy and Rand shortly after Mercaniad rises tomorrow."

Immediately the Guardian group left, Kirk took out his communicator and flipped it open. "*Enterprise,* this is Kirk. Let me speak with Mister Spock."

"Spock here, Captain."

"Things aren't going as well as expected, Mister Spock."

"Indeed? It appears that the system's star is getting ready to drastically increase its stellar constant."

"Aha! So you found out about that independently?"

"Of course, Captain. The normal monitoring of the stellar wind, the gravitational pulsing, the neutrino flux, and the density of the flocculi are standard measurements of stellar instability. These data plus other factors permit me to estimate that the probability of the star undergoing an unstable phase is almost unity."

"Do you have any estimate of the possible intensity of the flare-up, Spock?"

"Negative, sir. It appears that there will be moderate increases in the emissivity of the star in the infrared, visible light, and ultraviolet wavelengths. I'm not certain of any increase in gamma radiation. However, some of the data are unusual because I've not been able to correlate them with any radiation that is normally produced by a Class G star."

"There may be a lot of things about Mercaniad that are unusual because it got bounced around in that space fold, Spock."

"True, Captain, but I haven't been able to ascertain any increased radiation levels beyond those I mentioned . . . and they shouldn't be of a level that will cause permanent harm to humanoid life forms, although surface conditions may become uncomfortable from an environmental point of view."

"Well, Spock, let me know, because Scotty and I

have been banished from the protective Keeps, although they're going to let McCoy and Yeoman Rand into the Keeps as experimental controls. . . ."

"I take it, sir, that they didn't believe your story and that they've decided to experiment upon you as unusual life forms?"

"As you would say, quite correct. Is there any possibility that this stellar flare-up will damage the *Enterprise?*"

"I need to confer with Mr. Scott, Captain. I'm not certain that we have enough power in the remaining dilithium crystals."

"Scotty, confer with Mister Spock on your communicator," Kirk remarked. He listened for a moment as the engineer talked with the Science Officer. What he heard was not encouraging.

Finally Scott reported to Kirk, "Spock and I agree, based on the data he's relayed to me. The ship's shields will certainly withstand the increased stellar radiation from the infrared up through the gamma rays, provided the intensity increase in orbit doesn't exceed a five-times increase for more than fifty hours. Beyond that point, we begin to drain the remaining dilithium reserves rapidly."

"Do we have enough reserves to move the *Enterprise* far enough away from Mercaniad to get it out of danger if Mercaniad's radiation should exceed that level and duration?" Kirk asked.

"Negative, Captain," Spock's voice came back through the communicator. "Such a maneuver would gravely deplete the remaining dilithium crystals that we'll absolutely require to return to the Orion Arm, where we *may* be able to call for assistance from Star Fleet Command."

"Unless we can find dilithium crystals here on Mercan," Scott added.

The situation was getting more difficult all the time. The Guardians and their Proctors were going to split up his landing party, which would mean that the Guardians would have two hostages—Janice Rand and McCoy. He and Scotty, with Orun's help, could probably manage to survive the Ordeal, even if it meant transporting up to the ship when it got too bad on the surface of Mercan. But not even Spock was certain that the ship would survive the flare-up of Mercaniad if the star became too energetic or if the flare-up lasted too long. And there was no way to know at this time.

Plus there was some strange data that not even Spock could evaluate concerning the forthcoming flare-up, data that could make things worse.

"Spock, can the transporter room lock on this signal? We may have to get Yeoman Rand and Doctor McCoy out of here, regardless of the circumstances with the Guardians. Scotty and I have to stay here, on the assumption that the Technic is going to attempt a rescue during or before the Ordeal." It was a decision that Kirk didn't like to make, but he felt he couldn't afford to have his landing party split up, putting his Medical Officer and a woman member of his crew in the hands of the Guardians and Proctors in an unknown place, the Keeps. . . . At least, not while some of the Guardians believed them to be animals and therefore suitable for vivisection.

"Captain," Spock replied from the *Enterprise,* "you're surrounded by so much transporter activity on the surface in your present location that Lieutenant Kyle can't hold dematerialization lock on any of you. And this transporter activity appears to be increasing."

"There's going to be a lot of transporter activity down here in the next twenty-four hours, Spock. The powers-that-be are moving the whole population of the planet into the deep Keeps underneath the oceans, using the planetary transporter system."

"I have the transporter room on heel-to-toe watches

and Yellow Alert," Spock replied. "We'll attempt to get de-mat locks on you and hold them for as long as we can under the circumstances, Captain. But you must realize that we may not be able to transport immediately at any given time."

"We'll keep that in mind, Mister Spock. But I'm also concerned about some of that unusual data you've picked up coming from Mercaniad. Any further analysis on it?"

"Negative, Captain."

"Very well, speculate. What does it look like?"

"Nothing I have seen from a Class G star," the Science Officer reported. "But it bears some resemblance to some of the rare and little-understood emissions that come from some Class K stars. . . ."

"Jim," Bones McCoy, who had been listening to the conversation next to Kirk, said seriously, "that sounds like Berthold Rays. . . ."

"You may be right, Doctor McCoy," Spock's voice replied.

"But from a Class G star, they may have effects we don't know about. Berthold Rays themselves are bad enough!" McCoy added. "Incapacitation after several hours' exposure, followed by tissue disintegration during the agonal period, followed by death within seventy-two hours."

"If that's true," Scotty put in, "it means that the people aboard the *Enterprise* are in trouble, because that's *hard* radiation, and it takes a lot of shield power to stop it. We may not have enough."

The situation was indeed deteriorating. Kirk had a last-ditch course of action, one that he was *extremely* reluctant to take. He *could* shift into the "conquistador mode," putting on a show of force with the phasers of the *Enterprise* and perhaps even bringing down the shuttle craft. He didn't want to do that. He *had* to work something out because the Mercans could be far too important to the Federation. In addition, the prohibition against a flagrant violation of General Order Number One ran deep within him. The Prime Directive is violated only in the most extreme cases, when all alternatives have failed.

All of the alternatives hadn't failed yet, but they were disappearing rapidly.

Chapter Eight

"Captain Kirk, I am *not* going to go with those Proctors to some suboceanic cave as an experimental animal unless you give me a direct order to do so," Yeoman Janice Rand said firmly.

"Neither am I, Jim," McCoy added. "What kind of nonsense is this, anyway? As a doctor, *I'm* the one who's supposed to do the biopsies and autopsies, not the other way around."

"James Kirk, I'm certain the Technic is aware of our predicament," Orun put in. "Delin and Othol have undoubtedly given their full reports by now, and we may even be under surveillance by the Technic. They may be waiting for the proper opportunity to come to us with traveler controls so that we may join them in our own Keeps . . . which are a great improvement over those of the Guardians and Proctors because of what we've learned about the nature of the Ordeal. . . ."

Kirk made up his mind right then. "We're not going to let Pallar and Lenos split us up," he stated flatly. "In the first place, we're a team, and that's why each of you was selected for this landing. Second, if the Technic does attempt to make contact with us as Orun claims they will, I want all of us to be there . . . and I *do not* want to have to search a whole planet to find the other half of my landing party."

It was a direction that Kirk didn't want to take, but the actions of the Guardians in not accepting even part of the truth of his story were forcing him in that direction. However, he began to see new options opening up for him as a result. He would have to walk a fine line between the conquistador and the diplomat, but his new options did permit him to utilize all of the power that he'd reluctantly held in check up to that point.

"Right now," Kirk went on, "we're going to stop being cooperative. We're going to start giving the Guardians some problems . . . and that means making ourselves very hard to find. The next step in the process is making ourselves very difficult to handle for the Proctors." He pulled his hand phaser from under his tunic. "Everyone, check phasers on stun . . . and we use them if the Proctors try to stop us."

"Now you're talking!" Scotty put in with a smile.

"I was beginning to wonder what it would take to bring you back to being Captain James T. Kirk," Bones McCoy added. "You certainly waited long enough to take action. I was getting a little bit worried about you, Jim."

Kirk ignored McCoy's comments. "Orun, I take it the Proctors have no real way of locating us if we leave here," Kirk questioned their Mercan companion.

"That's true. They'll have to search for us, but they can do it by traveling to many places quickly, completing a search that would otherwise take a long period if they had to walk."

"We'll still make it as difficult as possible for them. How about the Technic? Will they have the same trouble finding us?"

"I don't think so, but I don't know everything that the Technic possesses in this regard. . . ."

"Which means that they *can* locate us if they want to," Kirk snapped. "All right, everyone, let's go.

Orun, lead the way and take us to a place that they won't think to look for us."

Kirk was back in action, and his landing party was glad of it.

As they left the villa, Kirk flipped open his communicator. *"Enterprise,* this is Kirk."

"Uhura here, Captain."

"Inform Mister Spock that we're leaving our host's villa. They're threatening to split us up. We're going to make ourselves hard to find, so even Spock may have trouble locating our coordinates."

"He's already having trouble, sir," the Communications Officer's voice reported. "The transporter activity on the planet is increasing rapidly."

"It's going to slack off by sunset, Celerbitan time, Uhura. By that time, the population will be in the Keeps, and Mercaniad will be well along into its current phase of instability. We'll keep in touch. Kirk out."

Captain's Log, supplemental, stardate unknown, inputted on a tricorder somewhere on the Mercan city-island of Celerbitan.

It's not easy to hide from Proctors. They seem to be everywhere in Celerbitan, passing the word to people and urging them to transport into the Keeps. The Keep for Celerbitan appears to be in the depths of a very large ocean called Sel Ethan directly south of this island chain. As a result of our uniforms and our different appearance, we're holed up in what appears to be a large warehouse full of pallets, boxes, and other packed goods in the foothills north of the main city and the Guardian Villa. Orun suggested that we obtain some Mercan clothing, but I vetoed this because there's no way that we can look like Mercans, even in their simple loose-fitting clothing. We're just too short for anyone to mistake us for Mercans. It's time and effort that would have been wasted anyway, because even if we were taken as Mercans, the Proctors would try to herd us into the Keep . . . and there we'd certainly be discovered. We're well hidden now, and most of the local population of this area has been evacuated already. We have water in a stream that runs past this warehouse and through a semitropical forest outside, so we can hold on for quite some time with our emergency rations. However, Orun fully expects us to be contacted by the Technic before sunset tomorrow. As far as we know, the Proctors haven't followed us here. Our tricorders show no life-form activity within a kilometer or so that would indicate Proctor presence.

Another supplemental report, sundown, one Mercan day before the Guardians predicted the start of the Ordeal. Looking at Mercaniad through the haze of the ocean air on the horizon, it becomes quite apparent that something is happening to the star. It has sun spots large enough to be seen with the naked eye. Even at the bottom of this atmosphere it's possible to see extensive prominences beginning to extend from the photosphere around its disc. I don't think anyone has watched the antics of a Class G irregular variable at this range before. I hope Mister Spock is getting copious data.

Spock was. Kirk's communicator whistled at him about midnight, awakening him from a rather fitful sleep on some fluffy plasticlike bags of fiber product stored in one part of the warehouse. He pulled out his communicator, flipped it open, and told it softly, "Kirk here."

"Spock, Captain. I have some bad news."

"I've been afraid of that, Mister Spock. But give me the specifics."

"The stellar activity is increasing at a much greater rate than I'd anticipated or than the computer had calculated on the basis of available data. We have thirty hours and seventeen-point-five minutes until the stellar activity will theoretically peak, and it may hold that intensity for as long as sixty-two hours, plus or minus forty hours as a three-sigma value. The maximum stellar activity will raise the spectral classification of Mercaniad to Class F1 . . . far above our original expectations. . . ."

"That's trouble," Scotty's voice came through the gloom of the darkened warehouse near Kirk. He moved over toward Kirk. "That'll drain our power reserves to the critical point. We canna make it through with the *Enterprise* at this distance from the star."

"Quite correct, Mister Scott," Spock's voice came back, emotionless as usual. "There is only one chance in four thousand nine hundred and eighty-seven-point-nine-five that the shields of the *Enterprise* will offer sufficient protection for the crew, and we can anticipate at least two-thirds of the crew being overcome. It is not simply a matter of electromagnetic spectrum radiation from the infrared through gamma rays, Captain. The unusual radiation you ordered me to speculate about earlier is now increasing to the point where I can begin to analyze it."

"Berthold Rays, Mister Spock?" Kirk wanted to know.

"Not precisely, since Berthold Rays have been known to emanate only from Class K stars," the Science Officer went on. "It appears to be a far more energetic form of Berthold radiation with a very high energy content."

Kirk discovered that McCoy was also awake now and at his other side. "Which means that the effects will be intensified, and that the agonal period will not only occur sooner but be more traumatic," the doctor put in. "That's enough to fry us for certain, except in a very deep cave, and it certainly isn't going to be healthy for anybody on the ship, Jim."

"And celestial mechanics won't let us just park the ship in orbit in the shadow of the planet for that long. Mercan has no natural satellite and no Lagrangian points." There appeared to be only one option now open to the captain of the star ship *Enterprise*. "Spock, as quickly as you can get *any* sort of transporter lock on us, beam us all up. We'll simply have to use the energy to pull us away from Mercaniad until things calm down. When and if they do, we'll have to deal with the Mercans in the best way that we can at that time. But I will *not* risk the lives of the crew and the safety of the ship. Mister Spock, five to beam up."

He started to get to his feet, and the others followed suit, assuming locations for transporting. Janice Rand awakened Orun and pointed out where he was to stand.

"Captain, I believe there is an alternative," Spock's voice came back. "This star is in a transition state at the moment. There's one chance in seventeen-point-three that we may be able to dampen the intensity of its flare-up, and one chance in three hundred fourteen-point-seven-nine that we may be able to stabilize it permanently as a Class G0 star."

"What do you have in mind, Spock?"

"My analysis indicates that an additional energy input of quite small proportions—a trigger effect, as it were—will damp the runaway nuclear and gravitational surges within the star," the Vulcan reported. "Captain, I propose to put two photon torpedoes into Mercaniad, one at each stellar pole simultaneously, with each traveling at Warp Factor Two. Those torpedoes will be deep within the star before the star can react to them. I will fuse the photon torpedoes for delayed detonation so their energy release occurs deep in the stellar core. . . ."

"You spoke of a very long chance that it would dampen the activity, Spock. What are some of the other possibilities?" Kirk queried, because he had detected a note of hesitancy in Spock's voice that only he, the Captain, would have noticed because of years of close association with the half-Vulcan/half-human.

Spock was silent for a moment. "There is one chance in four hundred and ten-point-three that the photon torpedoes will cause Mercaniad to nova. . . ."

"I don't like those odds, Mister Spock. We're almost better off doing nothing at all rather than trying to tickle an irregular variable star."

"Sir, as I stated, there is an excellent chance that this action will dampen this stellar flare-up. The chances of causing the star to either stabilize or nova are of the same order of magnitude, but are far greater than damping it. Your alternative, sir, is to beam aboard so that we can withdraw and return when the flare-up is over. . . ."

Kirk was used to making decisions firmly and expeditiously when necessary. He'd been evaluating the options in his mind even as Spock reported to him and proposed the star-busting operation. In view of what he felt he had to do—get his ship repaired, which would require the assistance of the Mercans, which in turn would mean bringing them into the Federation if they would come—he came to a decision.

"Belay the order to beam up, Spock. You're authorized to attempt to torpedo Mercaniad. However, do it before local sunrise here and be prepared to beam us up on a moment's notice and jump at once to maximum possible Warp Factor if you do succeed in triggering a nova."

"I will have to compute the optimum time to dispatch the photon torpedoes, Captain. It may not be possible to do the job before the star is in your local sky down there. However, as I told you, creating a nova is the slimmest chance of all. But you can be assured that I will take whatever actions are necessary to save both the landing party *and* the ship, should something go awry."

"I'm sure you will, Mister Spock," Kirk told the communicator.

"He will," McCoy put in. He knew the Vulcan, too. Spock wasn't a conniving First Officer eager to assume command. He disliked command as much as Kirk relished it.

"Do I have your permission to proceed with the launching of two photon torpedoes at Mercaniad at my discretion, Captain?"

"Yes, Mister Spock, you do. Keep me informed."

"And just remember, Spock, we're down here on the surface without the ship's shielding that you enjoy," McCoy snapped.

"I presume that was Doctor McCoy," Spock's transmission replied. "Please remind him that the ship's shielding isn't going to do any of us up here any good whatsoever if the torpedoing does not work. . . . But also remind him that I do not intend to fail. Spock out."

Orun was more than interested in the communicators. "I've heard you speak into those little devices, James Kirk, and I've heard them speak back to you. I haven't questioned you, since I was afraid that my interest would arouse the interest of the Guardians or Proctors. What are they? Small calculators that reply to you verbally instead of by digital or analog display?"

"I'll bet that your ancestors had them once," Kirk remarked. He showed his communicator to Orun. "If I was on the other side of Celerbitan, and you wanted to talk to me, what would you do?"

"Why, I would simply use my traveler control to query the Central Directory concerning your location, and then I would merely travel to where you happened to be," the Mercan replied.

"Suppose you didn't have your traveler-control unit? Suppose you were caught as we are now without your traveler control? How would you talk to me?" Kirk persisted.

"I would not. I could not," Orun told him bluntly.

"Ah, but we can. Since we don't have travelers of the sort you use here on Mercan—ours are of a different type—we've developed these communication units to permit us to talk to each other instead of traveling to see one another when we want to talk. It saves a lot of time."

"But who are you talking to?"

"To another person like myself in the traveling device that brought us to Mercan." Kirk flipped open the communicator. *"Enterprise,* this is Kirk. When is your next pass over the island chain where we are located, Uhura?"

"One moment, Captain. Let me check with Lieutenant Sulu. . . . Approximately five minutes, Captain."

"Thank you, Uhura. Kirk out." He snapped the cover shut and replaced it under his tunic. "Orun, come outside. I want to show you something."

The diurnal convection clouds that brought rain to Celerbitan in the early hours of every morning hadn't yet started to form. The sky was still relatively clear outside the warehouse. Stretched across the sky was the Orion Arm of the Galaxy, a murky river of wan light whose individual stars weren't visible to the naked eye. Kirk watched with Orun for a moment. Then he pointed off to the southwest. "There. Do you see it?"

A bright, gleaming point of light was moving southwest to northeast across the sky at an angle of about five degrees to the equator.

Much as Kirk was in control of himself, a lump arose in his throat when he saw that moving point of light. There she was, the *Enterprise.* And here he was on the ground. Unless he could manage to work things out down here, his ship was in trouble . . . perhaps even doomed.

Orun had a different reaction to seeing the moving light in the sky. It was probably the very first time he had ever seen *anything* moving in the night sky of

Mercan. "It . . . it is hard to believe!" he whispered as he stood there watching the *Enterprise* move across the Mercan night sky in its standard orbit. "I . . . I have believed your story, James Kirk, because it's in concert with things that I wanted to believe . . . things that we were discovering from our own searching into the ways of the Universe. . . . But it's different to actually see something like this and to *know* that what we believe is probably true. . . ."

"Son, I know how you feel." It was McCoy's gentle voice from behind them. "Sometimes it's difficult to accept the fact that dreams and beliefs can come true. When the world turns out the way you want it to, it's sometimes more frightening than if it had stayed the way it was."

"Aye." It was Scotty's voice. "Be careful what you ask for, because you'll get it. . . . " In the gloom, Kirk could see that his engineer was watching the bright light of the *Enterprise* pass across the sky with a wistful longing of his own. Star Fleet people are rarely at home on planets. . . .

"Will your traveling device come back over?" Orun wanted to know when the *Enterprise* disappeared below the horizon.

"Every two hours," Kirk said, but his Translator broke down on that statement because, as Scotty had pointed out, the Mercan language had no time reference in its structure other than terms for indefinite time periods.

Orun looked around furtively. "I think we had better get back inside," he warned. "The Proctors have devices that can sense our body heat. If they're looking for us, they'll be doing it with infrared sensors."

"Bones, any sign of activity on the tricorder?" Kirk asked.

"Negative, Jim. Nothing except a few small life forms in the thicket over there."

"Orun's right, Captain. If the Proctors have infrared

sensors, we're sitting ducks out here in the open. At least the building there masks our body-heat signatures," Scotty pointed out.

Back in the warehouse, Kirk decided they'd have to do more than just hide out there. They'd have to be prepared to detect any Mercan approaching the warehouse in the night, and they'd also have to be prepared to defend themselves against Proctors if necessary. "We've been lax on our security . . . especially since we're fugitives right now," he said. "Bones, can you set up for an omnidirectional life-forms scan on your tricorder with an alarm that will alert us if anybody comes near?"

"I think I can do that, Jim."

But nothing happened for the rest of the night. Kirk managed only a fitful sleep, anticipating the imminent beeping alarm of McCoy's tricorder at any moment. It seemed strange to him that the Proctors were apparently so ineffectual that five fugitives couldn't be quickly located and apprehended. He thought about this as he tossed and turned, and it finally occurred to him that the Proctors were probably more pomp, show, and bluster than an effective police force. Kirk had gathered that the Guardians had considerable political power over the people of Mercan because of the Guardian possession of the Mystery of the Ordeal—the ability to predict the flare-ups of the Mercaniad irregular variable star. This ability to predict natural activities of a life-and-death nature to all Mercan life would indeed bring in its wake inevitable political power.

The Mercan culture, with its easy access to travel around this world, had enabled the Guardians to unify the planet as Kirk had rarely seen before. It was a classic case of One World, one people, one culture, and one political power base—just like Earth and Vulcan.

But as a result, the Mercans were so unified by their Code, by their obvious social need for the combined astronomical predicting and judicial activities of the Guardians, and the occasional police activity of the

Proctorate, the Proctorate itself had almost degenerated into an organization whose only real function was to maintain a show of force.

Mercanians were far too law-abiding.

When Kirk came to that conclusion, it answered a lot of questions about their treatment since arriving on Mercan.

No Mercan could conceive of walking away from a house arrest. It was just unthinkable.

Which meant that the Proctors were perhaps less of a force to be reckoned with than Kirk's own cultural bias had originally been willing to admit. The Proctors were *not* a planet-bound version of Star Fleet. In essence, the Proctors were just the Palace Guard, the remnants of a true military force backing up a political force. Once the political force was so firmly consolidated, the real need for the Proctorate became less. The Proctors were one step away from being ceremonial in nature.

And that, in turn, explained to Kirk's satisfaction why the Guardians appeared to be so inept and so confused in their handling of their newly arisen competition, the Technic. They just didn't really remember how to consolidate power once they had it. Their Guardian power had been uncontested for so long that they took it almost for granted. The Guardians couldn't handle the upstart Technic—whoever they might be— because other than Orun, Kirk had no positive knowledge that such group even existed on Mercan.

Dawn came like a blast furnace.

There was no question in anyone's mind that the Ordeal was about to commence and that it would be an ordeal indeed.

It grew very hot very quickly as Mercaniad rose above the horizon.

"Jim," McCoy pointed out, monitoring the output of his tricorder, "if something doesn't happen pretty quick, we're in big trouble. Spock is right: that star is emitting a very powerful form of Berthold Rays. If we don't get some shielding between us and that star within a matter of hours, we might as well forget the whole thing."

Kirk shook his head in frustration. His options were rapidly disappearing again. He couldn't wait for the invisible Technic; they might not show up at all. He couldn't count on Spock's actions in torpedoing Mercaniad; it might occur too late to save the party on the ground from the lethal effects of the radiation from Mercaniad. He *had* to get his landing party and Orun back to the *Enterprise,* where they had *some* shielding.

"*Enterprise,* this is Kirk. Spock, we're getting a bellyful of these hyper-Berthold Rays down here," Kirk snapped into his communicator. "When are you scheduled to torpedo Mercaniad?"

"Optimum time would appear to be in ten hours and forty minutes, Captain."

"That's too long. We'll fry down here. Beam us up."

"Captain, transporter activity on the Island of Celerbitan has increased again with the coming of sunrise there," Spock reported from the ship. "There's so much activity that we may not be able to beam you up at all."

"Have him get down to the transporter room himself," Scotty suggested. "Between Spock and Kyle, there's not two people on the *Enterprise* right now that know more about the transporter!"

"Mister Scott, I *am* in the transporter room now," Spock's voice came back. "We are trying to lock on you. We can't get a scan-lock."

"I'll take my chances down here on Mercan with Berthold Rays rather than get scrambled in a bad transporter beaming," McCoy growled. "Unless Spock gets a clear lock, beam up without me. It's bad enough to go through that thing when it's working right."

"As a matter of fact, Captain," Spock's voice went on as though McCoy had been completely ignored, "there is strong transporter activity in the immediate vicinity of your signal at this moment. I would suggest an immediate tricorder life-form scan around you at once, because something is beaming into your area now. And I can't beam you out under those circumstances."

Through the walls of the warehouse, Kirk heard the ringing song of a transporter/traveler materialization.

Chapter Nine

Spock's words galvanized Kirk into action.

"Phasers out and on stun," Kirk snapped, pulling his phaser from beneath his tunic. "Rand, Bones, tricorder sweep. Where are they?"

"Outside the building, Captain," Janice Rand reported, swinging her tricorder around.

"How many?"

"Three of them, sir."

"Do we take up defensive positions in here?" Scott wanted to know.

"No, they might burn this place down around us. They're still materializing, so they aren't organized yet. We'll attack before they get the chance." Kirk headed toward one of the big doors to the warehouse. "Rand, McCoy, cover Scotty and me. We'll go for the stream and get them in cross fire. Once we're down, we'll cover for you."

Although Kirk was in a lighter gravity field than standard, he discovered that he didn't move faster than Orun, who beat him to the door, his Mercan single-shot firearm drawn and ready to blast away for effect if necessary. The Mercan assumed a crouch in the doorway, firearm held out in front of him with both hands, ready to fire.

But Orun dropped his gun to his side, then holstered it just as Kirk and Scott got ready to make their dash through the door to the streambed.

"James Kirk, hold! Our visitors are Delin and Othol with a Technic leader!" Orun shouted. "They've come, just as I knew they would."

Kirk held up his hand to his landing party and did not put his phaser away. "Orun, check them. Make certain they're alone. This could be a Proctorate trap."

"It's no trap," Orun told him. "Not with a prominent Technic leader in the group." The tall Mercan walked out into the glaring sunlight toward the group of three Mercans which was approaching the warehouse from the forest margin near the stream.

"Whew!" McCoy breathed a sigh of relief. "Talk about the cavalry coming over the hill to the rescue at the last moment. . . ."

"You're an incurable romanticist, Bones," Kirk remarked, securing his phaser as he saw for himself that it was indeed the rescue group that Orun had forecast.

"Well, perhaps not at the last moment," the doctor added, correcting himself. "But another couple of hours in this growing Berthold radiation would have made it the last moment."

Kirk flipped open his communicator. "*Enterprise,* this is Kirk. Spock, the transporter activity you detected was a group of three of their technical people coming to rescue us."

"Thank you for reporting, Captain. We were getting ready to beam you out of there," Spock's voice replied.

"I don't think that will be necessary now, Spock. We've made contact here with the group that has the best chance of being able to help Scotty."

"Very well, sir, but there is still considerable transporter activity going on within a ten-kilometer radius of your location, although not enough to prevent us from obtaining a good transporter lock on you. Prudence dictates that we maintain readiness here to beam up a large party if necessary," the First Officer of the *Enterprise* suggested.

"Logical, Spock."

"Of course, Captain."

"Kirk, come!" Orun called out to them.

"Keep this channel open, Spock." He turned to Janice Rand. "Yeoman, keep your communicator open to Spock. Secure phasers, everyone. Let's go meet our rescuers."

Kirk recognized the woman Delin and the other young Mercan, Othol, both of whom had been present at their original beam-down site. They greeted the Federation party with palms up, the Mercan sign of welcome. A tall Mercan man, obviously older than the rest, with thinning head hair and a spotty loss of protective skin coloring on his high cheekbones and other prominent high points of his face, extended his palms up to Kirk. "Welcome, James Kirk. And welcome to your companions. I am Thallan of the Technic Peers. Please accept the apologies of the Technic for not coming to your aid before this, but we could not do so without creating a confrontation with the Proctorate. . . ."

"Your apologies are accepted, Thallan," Kirk told him, offering him palms up in return. He started to introduce the remainder of his landing party, when Thallan interrupted.

"We know of them, James Kirk. Formal introductions should wait until we have traveled to the safety of our private Keep under Eronde," the Technic leader said. "We dare not stay out here too long because Mercaniad is becoming more active every moment. We're also in danger of the Proctorate discovering our traveling here, in spite of their heavy activity in getting the populace into the Keeps. . . ."

He handed a small device to Kirk while Orun distributed others to the Federation landing party. Kirk recognized it as a Mercan traveler control. "Thallan, we're not from Mercan. We don't know how to operate these."

Thallan nodded. "As I had expected from Othol's report. Very well, if you'll follow my instructions, we'll travel to our Keep. . . ."

The Technic leader's brief lecture on operation of the Mercan transport-control unit was interrupted by the ringing sound of multiple transporter materializations around them.

Within seconds, the entire group was surrounded by nine armed Proctors who materialized with weapons drawn and ready.

Prime Proctor Lenos himself materialized not five meters from Kirk and Thallan.

"Long life to you, Thallan. And to Othol and Delin as well," Lenos said with just a touch of mockery in his voice. "We knew that if we waited long enough, you'd rise to the bait in this trap and attempt to save your Technic constructs. Now, hand me your traveler controls, all of you. We are going to travel together, but not to Eronde."

"Proctor Lenos, you have no right under the Code to detain us," Thallan protested, making no move to surrender his traveling control.

"I'm operating under a warrant from the Guardian One to detain these four Technic constructs and any Mercan who is accompanying them," Lenos replied in less than cordial tones, the cultured mannerisms of Mercan slipping away under the increasing emotional strain of the encounter. "They've made insane statements to the Guardian Group leaders concerning the truth of the Code of the Abode and the accepted legends of the Beginning. Hand me your traveling control. . . ."

"They're not Technic constructs, nor are they part of the Technic group, Lenos," Thallan replied, still holding his control. "I haven't seen them before and know of them only what Othol and Delin here have reported to me."

"They're not from the Abode, Lenos," Orun repeated. "I've told the Guardian One this fact. He doesn't believe me."

"This is why *all* of you must travel with me," Lenos commanded. "You are all afflicted with this insanity and will require retraining. We will travel with you all to the Retraining Keep, where you'll be examined by the Guardians and subjected to retraining . . . except that your deformed constructs here will be used for medical studies. . . ."

Insofar as Kirk was concerned, this was getting out of hand again very quickly, and the Proctorate trap he'd feared had now been sprung and was leading them into a worsening situation. In addition, it was getting *hot!* Beads of sweat stood out on the faces of the other three members of his party, and sweat ran down his own face and into the corners of his eyes, making it difficult for him to see without rubbing his eyes. Now he knew why the Mercans wore the headbands. . . .

It was a situation in which he was going to have to act.

Kirk turned his head to Janice Rand, who was standing next to him. "Do you have the comm channel open?"

"Yes, sir."

Kirk stepped between Lenos and Thallan and looked up at the armored Proctor, who towered above him. "Lenos, it is time I proved to you that I'm right!" He called loudly so that Janice Rand's communicator would pick up his voice, hoping as he did so that Lenos wouldn't overreact. Lenos didn't; he merely stared in disbelief as Kirk spoke. "*Enterprise,* this is Kirk. Spock, beam down immediately. Transporter crew, stand by to beam the entire group back aboard on my command."

He was counting on Spock's disciplined mind to follow orders precisely and immediately . . . and he was not disappointed.

Almost at once, there was the ringing of the transporter beam from the *Enterprise* off to his left. He hadn't noticed before, but there was a slight difference in the sound between the Mercan traveler and the Federation transporter unit.

Spock appeared, his gaunt form almost as tall as the Mercans around him but with his upswept eyebrows and pointed ears a definite and obvious difference. Spock had not only acted immediately but also anticipated Kirk's command, because he had a tricorder slung over his shoulder and a Type II hand phaser nestled in his right hand.

"Ladies and gentlemen of Mercan, permit me to introduce the First Officer of the star ship *Enterprise* and my second-in-command, Mister Spock from Vulcan . . . *another* abode of life," Kirk announced with exaggerated politeness.

Thallan was obviously surprised by this appearance of the Vulcan, but his expression slowly turned into one of excitement and pleasure as he drew his lips back in a Mercan smile.

On the other hand, Proctor Lenos appeared confused. He looked at Thallan, then at Kirk, then at Spock. "How did you do that?" Lenos asked in disbelief. "We've put a traveling blockage in the central traveler-control system to prevent anyone from traveling here except with *my* traveler code."

"There's a slight difference in the way our traveler works, Lenos," Kirk put in, taking a guess.

"Quite correct," Spock added. "We detected the suppressor field and were able to phase around it. And we're ready in the ship, Captain, to take whatever action is necessary."

Kirk took out his phaser and signaled his party to do the same. "All of you will travel with *us*. We have a Keep in the sky, our traveling device which is going around the Abode at this time. Lenos, you and your Proctors will please give us your firearms at once."

"*We* are the Proctors here! *We* give the orders! Not you!" Lenos snarled, reaching for his sidearm. "Proctors! Fire on this construct!"

The Proctors didn't have a chance. One of them raised his multi-round long-barreled pistol, but that was as far as he got. Spock reacted first.

The Proctor dropped to the ground, stunned into unconsciousness by Spock's phaser bolt.

By that time, Scotty and Janice Rand had dropped four of the other Proctors in the squad, using the stun setting on their hand phasers.

Kirk didn't even have time to react, so well-trained were his people.

There was absolute silence for a long moment while the reality of what they had just witnessed sank in for the remaining Mercan Proctors . . . and for the other Mercan people of the Technic group who were there.

"Thank you, Spock," Kirk said.

Spock was resetting his phaser. He merely raised his eyebrow.

"What . . . what happened to my Proctors?" Lenos stammered, lowering his firearm. The remaining three Proctors in his squad, seeing their leader do this, also lowered their weapons.

"They're merely unconscious. They'll be all right in a short while," Kirk said. "I told you we weren't from the Abode. I'm sorry that it took violence to demonstrate something to you that you could not believe. Now, hand us your weapons, Lenos. Thallan, if your Technic people will keep their weapons holstered, I won't require that you surrender."

"James Kirk, you and your companions are obviously *not* from the Abode, and you possess technical power in weaponry far beyond ours," the Technic leader said. "We're at your mercy, sir."

"On the contrary, you are our guests," Kirk replied smoothly. "And that includes you, Lenos. We've got seventeen to beam up, so we'll start with the Proctors first in groups of six. . . ."

As Kirk had expected, the Mercans were totally dazed when they materialized aboard the *Enterprise*. This gave the ship's security detachment time to step onto the transporter stage, one man to a Proctor.

"Put the Proctor squad in detention cabins," Kirk ordered. "Thallan, Orun, Othol, Delin, Lenos . . . please come with Commander Spock and me to the Bridge. Scotty, you've got work to do conserving power for our shields. Bones, find out what happened to Orun's blood sample and come to the Bridge with the details as soon as you have them."

"Right you are, Captain," Scotty murmured, and disappeared toward a turbolift that would take him to the Engineering Section.

"It's good to get back . . . and considerably cooler, too!" was McCoy's comment. "Now what's taken M'Benga so long with the analysis of that sample? . . ."

The Technic people seemed a good deal less overwhelmed by the star ship than Proctor Lenos, who gaped at everything. There was no question about it: there was fear in the Proctor's eyes. Kirk knew that the *Enterprise* was quite beyond the Proctor's comprehension. But both Orun and Delin actually seemed to be overjoyed at seeing the different technology around them in the star ship.

Kirk took them to the Bridge. As the turbolift doors opened, Spock immediately went to his library computer console. Kirk waved his hand around the Bridge. "Mercans, this is the control center for our traveling device."

"This is only a Technic mockery," Proctor Lenos objected. "Somehow, somewhere on the Abode, Thallan, you've managed to construct this very unusual Keep. I must congratulate you on doing a magnificent job. It's certainly much more comfortable than the Guardian Keeps . . . and shows evidence of a technology far greater than anything we or the Guardians had ever suspected."

Thallan was looking around, obviously impressed,

but in an intellectual sense rather than with the sense of fear and apprehension that Lenos was exhibiting. "Lenos, you know that I'm one of the oldest of the Technic group. You may not know that I sit on the Technic Peer Panel of Thirteen that provides advice and guidance to others who have declared for the Technic Belief. As a member of this Panel, I *know* what's being done on the Abode. Lenos, I speak the truth, *this is not of the Technic!*"

"But what else can it be?"

"Proctor Lenos, your mind is no different than mine except that I have been trained to accept and adapt to new ways, new things, and new thoughts," Thallan told him. "You've been trained to follow the orders of the Guardians without question and to accept their dogma . . . without question. You may have a difficult time accepting the reality of this change that has come to Mercan from the Ribbon of Light. You'll have to learn to accept this change . . . or you will no longer be able to function as Prime Proctor. In fact, all of us are going to have to learn how to accept some changes we never anticipated, even in our wildest heresies about the Code."

That, of course, was precisely what was worrying Captain James Kirk at the moment.

But in spite of his concern over the possibility of having violated General Order Number One, Kirk's first thoughts were of his command—the *Enterprise* and her crew, who were now in mortal danger, with very few options available. In fact, Kirk had had to narrow his range of options considerably by the pressure of events.

He did have a new option now, however. He had the Prime Proctor of Mercan aboard the *Enterprise,* for use, if not as a hostage, then as a bargaining point with Pallar and the rest of the Guardians once the immediate problems presented by the instability of Mercaniad were solved. And he'd had to bring aboard the star ship at least four intelligent, technically cognizant Mercan inhabitants, some of whom knew what they were seeing on the *Enterprise* and who'd be able to apply the Federation technology to the technology of Mercan once they returned to the planet. The point of no return had passed; there was no way that the *Enterprise* could ever leave Mercan, irrespective of how Scotty managed repairs, without leaving a permanent alteration of the Mercan culture behind. The door to any sort of unobtrusive visit had irrevocably closed behind Captain James T. Kirk.

Regardless of the internal conflict within him, Kirk had his priorities sorted out and knew what had to be done. If these priorities resulted in a flagrant violation of the Prime Directive, he was prepared to accept the consequences . . . even if it meant losing command of the star ship he had to save as his first priority.

"Mister Spock," he asked his Science Officer, leaving the Mercans for a moment and stepping over to where Spock was working with the library computer console, "what is the situation with Mercaniad?"

Spock did not divert his attention from the console. "Captain, I've been out of touch with the situation for several hours now because of the need to be present in the transporter room. I'm updating myself at this time. The best report I can provide right now is sketchy at best."

"Well, give me what you've got, Spock. What's that star doing?"

"Still increasing its emission constant across the entire electromagnetic spectrum and emitting an increasingly intense quantity of what could be termed hyper-Berthold Rays."

"How long before the ship's shielding might be compromised?"

"Unknown at present, since I have not been able to ascertain a definite trend because of instabilities even in the instabilities of this star," the Vulcan replied unemotionally. "It's the first Class G star of the irregular variable type that we've had the opportunity to investigate and observe, Captain. The other Class G stars of this type do not behave this way because they're accompanied by one or more very large gas-giant planets like Jupiter which produce a demonstrable effect because of gravitational attractions."

"Mister Spock, do I have hours before I must make a decision . . . or only minutes?"

Spock stopped his work at the console, looked up with his eyes focused on nothing in particular, and thought for a long moment before replying, "Captain, my best estimate indicates that you have seven-point-three hours before the radiation overcomes our shields. This is assuming, of course, that we're not able to launch the photon torpedoes into the star as planned before the radiation level becomes too great. . . ."

"Keep me informed, Mister Spock. If we have to use some of our precious power to pull back from Mercaniad, I want to know as soon as possible so we have time to evaluate all the options."

Spock's head was back in the hooded viewer of the library computer console. "Sir, you can rest assured that I will inform you of any data as quickly as I have it in hand."

Captain's Log: Stardate 5076.8

We can do nothing but wait for data from Spock's observations.

I gave the Mercans a quick tour of the ship after leaving the Bridge. The Prime Directive has already been compromised, and there was the chance that I might learn something more about the level of sophistication of these isolated people. I'm encouraged, but the Mercans may be learning more about us than we are about them.

Once Thallan discovered what Spock was doing, he and Othol began to cooperate with Spock, providing an unsuspected source of information on past Ordeals and the behavior of Mercaniad for the library computer to work on.

I didn't suspect that Orun knew enough physics to be of assistance to Commander Scott . . . but he has. Orun is down in Engineering with Commander Scott, advising the Engineering Officer of the exact nature of the radiation from Mercaniad so that the shields can be selectively adjusted to reject the most intense parts of the spectrum, thus saving power. Delin's in Sick Bay working with McCoy in the laboratory, assisting him in a complete biological work-up of the Mercans, donating her own blood and biopsy tissue samples as well as working alongside Doctor McCoy in the analysis, thus saving him considerable time.

These members of the Technic group on Mercan are intellectually brilliant people, and I wouldn't worry about the Prime Directive and about the possibility of bringing Mercan into the Federation if I were assured that all Mercans were of their quality of intellectual sophistication. These four are certainly our equals in many areas of science and technology, albeit sometimes from a totally different viewpoint and approach, as one might suspect from their isolation.

However, I know that all Mercans aren't like these four Technics. Having dealt with Pallar and his Guardian group, I frankly face a problem that I don't know how to solve, much less even how to approach at this time. It appears that the Guardians won't give up their dogma about being the sole abode of life in the universe. When these four Technics get back to Mercan with their acquired knowledge, they may feel strong enough to attempt to overthrow the Guardians. If this is the case, I may have triggered a planetary civil war . . . and I must take full responsibility for having done so if it occurs.

My big problem is Proctor Lenos, who appears

to be in a state of shock at the moment after seeing the *Enterprise*.

In fact, my biggest problem may be the Proctorate led by Lenos and even Lenos himself. He is *not* a stupid person. He may well convince himself of the reality of the *Enterprise* and of the subtle flaws in the Code that he's charged with enforcing. If he does come around, which way will he go and which way will he be able to take the Proctorate?

These must be considered as pure speculations inserted into the record merely to indicate the development of my own line of thinking as we proceed toward what appears to be an inevitable confrontation that will undoubtedly cause a drastic change in the culture of Mercan.

I have insufficient data to take action here at this time. In fact, I have insufficient data to act at all until Mister Spock reports. . . .

"Captain Kirk, Spock reporting," the intercom unit over Kirk's bed barked.

Kirk hadn't realized he'd been so tired. He'd just stretched out for a moment . . . but a quick look at his chronometer indicated he'd been asleep for several hours. Shaking his head groggily, he reached for the intercom reply switch. "Kirk here."

"Captain, can you come to the Bridge at once, please?"

"I'm on my way." Kirk didn't even bother to ask why. If Spock wanted him to come to the Bridge, it was because the Science Officer either had something he wanted to show to Kirk or something that he didn't wish to entrust to the security of the ship's intercom system.

It took Kirk less than a minute to get to Spock's side on the Bridge. Both Thallan and Othol were with Spock.

"Report, Mister Spock."

"Captain, request permission to launch the photon torpedoes at once, sir."

"Of course, Mister Spock. Why do you need my permission to take an action I've already approved?" Kirk wanted to know.

"Because of negligence on my part as the Science Officer," Spock replied without emotion.

"Negligence? Explain."

"Sir, I was called away from this station to provide the necessary assistance to the transporter crews for your rescue from the planetary surface," Spock explained. "During my absence from this post, the situation with Mercaniad's instability got beyond my control. It required all my time since beaming up from the planet, plus the assistance from the Technic people here, to bring myself and the library computer up-to-date on the Mercaniad situation. . . ."

"Spock, get to the point."

"I now have discovered that it's too late to damp the flare-up of Mercaniad by launching photon torpedoes into its core."

Chapter Ten

"What do you mean, Mister Spock?" Kirk asked. "Specify."

"Mercaniad progressed into its flare-up far more rapidly than I'd anticipated," the Science Officer explained. "Additional data provided to me by Thallan and Othol have now been analyzed by the ship's computer. I have performed an independent analysis by linearizing some of the data to simplify the equations. My results agree with those of the computer by a factor of two-point-three-nine percent, which is well within the limits of agreement one should anticipate utilizing the linearization methods I adopted."

Kirk mulled this over for a moment. Then he asked, "What would happen if we sent those torpedoes in there now?"

"May I have approximately two-point-four minutes to make the calculations, Captain? They're exceedingly complex because we are dealing with fusion reactions under very unstable conditions. . . ."

"Get busy, Spock. Time's running out," Kirk told him, and got out of his Science Officer's way, knowing better than to bother Spock at a time like this. He dropped into the command seat and punched the intercom button. "Mister Scott, this is Kirk. What are the latest estimates on the shielding?"

"Captain, I dinna know if she'll hold for another ten hours . . . which isn't enough to protect us all the way through the Ordeal . . . if Mister Spock's numbers are right . . . which they usually are. I can't keep these shields up enough to stop all those hyper-Berthold Rays, sir."

"Suppose you were to divert all available stand-by power into the shields, Scotty? Would they hold?"

"What would you like me to shut down, Captain?"

"As many internal systems as possible. As many absolutely nonessential circuits as you can drop off-line without getting us into a situation where we couldn't move in less than a few minutes' start-up time again. Drop the shields against ultraviolet; that won't get through the hull, no matter how strong it gets, and if it discolors the paint, so what? Drop the level against infrared, turn up the life-support temperature controls to the point where it endangers our electronics, and let us sweat a little bit if we have to."

"Aye, sir, will do! But that'll give us only about four more hours of protection. . . . And when we get through, we won't have enough power left aboard to boil water for tea."

"Scotty, just do the best you can . . . but maintain only enough shielding to keep us from being fried."

"It would help, Captain, if we could get nearly all the crew as far from the outer hull as possible," the Engineering Officer suggested. "Mass decreases the lethality of Berthold Rays. . . ."

"Thanks, Scotty, we'll work on that one." He switched off and directed his next question to his helmsman and Security Officer. "Mister Sulu, are you prepared to activate the maximum-radiation security procedure?"

"The 'storm-cellar' program? Yes, sir. But packing four hundred people into a space usually occupied by about fifty gets a little too cozy if we have to stay in there for more than twenty-four hours, sir. Sanitation gets to be a problem, too. . . ."

"It may be discomfort or death, Mister Sulu," Kirk reminded him.

"Yes, sir, I know that. We'll have to evacuate the Bridge for the maximum protection, Captain."

"I'm aware of that, Mister Sulu. What's the problem, since you were concerned enough to bring it to my attention?"

"We're getting a lot of stellar-proton and charged-particle flux, as well as electromagnetic radiation and hyper-Berthold Rays, sir. I'm having to ride herd manually every minute on all our automatic systems. One stellar proton through the shielding and through one of the picocircuits in the autopilot . . . and we could be into the atmosphere below in less than one orbit."

"So you're telling me that somebody's got to stay up here and monitor the automatic systems in the face of this extreme stellar storm, is that correct?"

"Yes, sir. And I'll stay."

Kirk thought about this for a moment. "No, Mister Sulu. 'Sacrifice' is not a word that's used in any of the Star Fleet Regulations . . . and it's not in my vocabulary, either. If it gets that bad, we won't stay here. Mister Chekov, plot a stand-by course of least-energy that will take us far enough from this blustering star for our shields to protect us."

"Aye, sir. I, too, would rather be alive and short on power than to just sit here and boil like a samovar," the navigator replied with a wry smile, then got down to work on plotting the course.

"Captain, I have numbers for your consideration now," Spock announced from the hooded viewer. "If we place two proton torpedoes into the core of Mercaniad precisely twenty-three-point-one minutes from now, there is one chance in five-point-three that the star will stabilize *or* damp its flare-up. The alternative is not an ordinary nova, sir, but a supernova beginning with a core collapse, progressing to a chromosphere and photosphere blow-away, and culminating with a total collapse into a neutron star that worsens into a black hole."

"Recommendations, Spock?"

"With those odds, Captain, I would prefer to defer any recommendations."

"No sporting blood, Mister Spock?" Sulu asked rhetorically.

"Mister Sulu, Vulcans do not gamble," Spock reminded him.

"But I have to," Kirk pointed out. "I don't like the odds, but I can't get better ones. If we go, we'll go in a blaze of glory. Otherwise, we've got a reasonable chance of making it." Kirk paused a moment. He knew that there were other factors involved, including an entire planet and its population of millions of humanoids with a unique and advanced civilization. They would survive the Ordeal in the safety of their suboceanic Keeps as they had done for uncounted generations. But the USS *Enterprise* and 430 people aboard her, accompanied by a small contingent of Mercans, would *not* survive. There was no time for a detailed analysis, nor time for any agonizing appraisal. The decision had to be made . . . and it had to be made *now*.

The situation facing James T. Kirk, star-ship Captain, Star Fleet, United Federation of Planets, was but one reason why there are so few citizens of the Federation who manage to ascend to the heights of Starship Command.

"Mister Sulu, arm and prepare to launch two photon torpedoes. Get fuze settings and course coordinates from Mister Spock. Execute immediately."

"Aye, sir."

"Data is on the weapon control bus," Spock announced.

"Launch when ready," Kirk said quietly, well aware

of what he'd just said. He was doing more than merely tinkering with the workings of a star; that could be far less explosive in the long run than the tinkering he was doing with a humanoid civilization, a tinkering he could no longer avoid.

"Data is loaded. On-board guidance read-back checks. Internal power." Sulu manipulated switches. "Fire One. . . . One away. Fire Two. . . . Two away."

The unmistakable sound of the launching of two photon torpedoes rang through the Bridge.

"Cross your fingers," Chekov muttered.

"Don't let Spock see you do it," Sulu said to him *sotto voce.*

"Uhura," Kirk said, turning his seat to face his Communications Officer. "Full library computer data dump into at least three courier drones and get them on their way toward the Orion Arm as rapidly as feasible. If this star goes supernova, I want some record of what we did running ahead of that shock wave so that a Federation ship may intercept it someday."

"Yes, sir. Shall I continue transmission of routine distress signals on all subspace channels?"

"By all means. Somebody may pick them up," Kirk remarked. "If Star Fleet Command doesn't know we're in trouble out here, they'll start wondering where we are eventually. They're going to ask questions about what happened to the *Enterprise,* and if they happen to detect a supernova out here, they'll come looking . . . if they don't already have something coming at Warp Factor Eight anyway. . . ."

"Courier drones have been launched, Captain."

"Thank you, Lieutenant. Spock, the situation on the torpedoes, please."

"Sensors are tracking both. They are both on course. Impact simultaneously at both stellar poles in . . . four-point-three minutes . . . and detonations will be nearly simultaneous with their entry at Warp Factor Two."

Kirk noticed Thallan and Othol standing beside

Spock now, both looking a bit bewildered. "Thallan, do you understand what we've just done?"

"Barely, James Kirk," the elder Technic replied. "Your Translator devices do not precisely convert the meanings of some words because they do not exist in our language. But I can manage to follow most of it. My biggest problem—and I'm certain Othol shares it—is the fact that I'm having some difficulty in adjusting my concepts of the Universe to fit in with what I'm seeing and hearing."

"Three-point-five minutes," Spock announced.

"We've launched devices toward Mercaniad that will penetrate the interior," Kirk attempted to explain. "Once inside, they will release a great deal of energy of a specific kind. If we've done it properly, if the computer is right, if all the data you've given us is correct, and if we have a considerable amount of luck—which is a word that doesn't translate for you, I know—the Ordeal will stop and Mercaniad will settle down into a stable condition hereafter. No more Ordeals. On the other hand, if everything that all of us know turns out to be wrong . . . or if we didn't do *everything* precisely right, Mercaniad will explode."

Thallan was silent for a moment. Then he asked, "If Mercaniad explodes, what will happen to the Abode?"

Kirk said nothing, just shook his head.

"You took that chance, a chance that you would destroy a whole planet, a whole people, a whole culture?" Othol wanted to know.

"I had no alternative. If your Guardians had cooperated, we might have worked out some arrangement that could have eliminated all of this," Kirk observed.

"Why did you come to Mercan in the first place?" Othol asked, suddenly angry. "We were developing whole new ways to live together. In three generations, we would have changed all of the Abode! Why did you interfere?"

"In three generations, you would have discovered what we already know," Spock added, "and you would be trying this yourself. As a matter of fact, your assistance to me has taught me that you already have all of the basic data to try it. You would have found some factor that would drive you to it."

"But you signed the death warrant on a whole planet without even asking us about it!" Othol persisted.

"Othol, that 'death warrant' includes everyone on this ship as well. I had no recourse but to make that decision. We didn't come here deliberately. We tried to interact with you in such a way that it would offer the least impact upon your way of life. But the powers-that-be on Mercan had closed minds. I'm sorry. Anyway, the chances are in favor of the action working," Kirk said. Inwardly, he didn't like it any better than Othol did. "Sometimes you don't have the luxury of time enough to do things your own way. Circumstances usually force your hand and change things, whether you want them to change right then or not."

"One minute," Spock announced.

"Sulu, give us the view of Mercaniad on the main screen," Kirk ordered.

Mercaniad was just rising over the limb of Mercan, the Abode of Life. As it came into full view, the disk of the star could be seen to be pulsating, sending out long streamers of filamentary prominence material. Its surface was mottled with sunspots. Invisible on the screen was the stream of charged particles which made up a greatly increased stellar wind. Without the shielding of the *Enterprise,* the human and humanoid life aboard her would have been blown out like the flame of a candle in a wind.

"Thirty seconds. Torpedoes on course. Sensors will lose them in ten seconds as they begin to enter the corona."

"I'm not certain that I like the idea of having a front-row seat for a possible supernova," Chekov muttered.

"Fifteen seconds. Do you intend to warn the crew, Captain?"

"Negative, Mister Spock. If it goes supernova, those of us right here will have only about two seconds to realize what's happened. We're all disciplined enough to expect the end at any moment among the stars. . . ."

"Zero. Torpedoes have penetrated Mercaniad," Spock announced.

The attention of everyone on the Bridge was riveted on the forward viewscreen, except for Spock, who had his face buried in the hooded viewer of the library computer console. Except for the throbbing of the internal systems of the star ship *Enterprise,* there was no sound on the Bridge.

There was no change in the visual appearance of the star on the viewscreen.

Kirk whirled in his seat and swarmed up to Spock's console. "Any change, Spock?"

Spock did not remove his face from the viewing hood. "Negative, Captain. The torpedoes released such a small amount of energy compared to that of a star that we'll not see any change for at least nine minutes. Even a Class G star is a very large mass and cannot change immediately . . . unless it goes supernova . . . which it has *not* done . . . and which it is not going to do after all, because it would have blown away its photosphere by this time."

There was a large sigh of relief that emanated from Ensign Chekov, but Sulu remained impassive as usual. Uhura, who was a bit more emotional, merely dropped her face into her hands as she closed her eyes.

Kirk slapped the Vulcan on the shoulder in obvious elation and relief. "You did it, Spock!"

Only at that point did the Vulcan remove his face from the viewing hood and querulously raise one eyebrow. "Sir, was there some doubt? The numbers were right. They had to be right. Mathematics is a logical science, Captain, and the logic of our calculations was indisputable. The probabilities were in favor of this outcome. I really do not understand this display of emotion, sir."

Kirk shook his head. "Spock, you're probably the first individual to tamper with a star knowing full well that it could blow us all away . . . and you managed to do it. I'll certainly see to it that this accomplishment of yours is properly entered in your record, along with a suitable commendation for cool-headed logic. . . ."

"Captain, how is it possible to thank logic?"

Kirk—and the rest of the crew of the *Enterprise* on the Bridge—couldn't suppress laughter, which was not directed at Spock's reply so much as it was a release of the incredible tension of the past few minutes.

It didn't take long after that to see that something was indeed happening to Mercaniad on the viewscreen. Spock switched spectral response to look at the star in both the ultraviolet and the X-ray wavelengths, then had a look at the stellar wind components and the stellar magnetic and gravitic fields. They were changing. It was patently obvious that Mercaniad was no longer pulsing, no longer shooting forth the stellar fireworks of prominences, and no longer increasing its output by spurts of activity, each greater than the last. It was settling down, pulsing occasionally, quieting slowly.

"Bridge, this is Engineering," Scotty's voice broke through the quiet activity of the control center. "Captain Kirk, the radiation level's dropping rapidly and the hyper-Berthold Rays now have a decreased intensity. If this keeps up, our screens are going to hold with no increase in power required to maintain protection. Don't tell me that Spock was wrong about Mercaniad?"

"Not at all, Scotty. As a matter of fact, Spock is now the only Star Fleet Science Officer who's managed to tickle a star and get away with it," Kirk replied with a smile.

"Did the photon torpedoes do the job?"

"They did indeed, Scotty. You can stand down from shield-monitoring alert now. Spock has probably got that errant star quieted down to a well-behaved Class G type."

"Orun says that's not possible," the engineer came back. "No Ordeal has been this short in duration."

"Tell him that things have changed, Scotty."

Captain's Log: Stardate 5077.5

Let the record show that it was the concept as well as the actions of Commander Spock, First Officer and Science Officer, to attempt to stabilize the irregular variable Class G star called Mercaniad by a triggering input of energy from two photon torpedoes. The chances of success were marginal, and the operation proceeded with my full authorization and with my full awareness of all of the possibilities, including those associated with the success of the venture. The able assistance and willful cooperation of three humanoid inhabitants of Mercan and members of their Technic group—Thallan, Othol, and Orun—were vital in the execution of this activity because they provided much of the long-term data on Mercaniad that was unavailable to Spock and the library computer. The behavior of Mercaniad during its flare-ups, locally termed the Ordeal by the Mercans, was also important data that was provided by the three Mercan experts.

Although the activity was conceived and carried through by Spock, it was done with my full authority, and I accept full responsibility for whatever the consequences may be.

A continuous watch on Mercaniad since the detonation of the photon torpedoes in its core has revealed that Spock's initial conclusions were correct. The star is rapidly stabilizing into what appears to be a regular Class G0 star with all the characteristics of stable Class G stars throughout our sector of the Galaxy. The output of hyper-Berthold Rays has diminished to practically zero;

complete data on this heretofore unreported phenomenon is stored in the library computer for later
analysis and interpretation by Federation stellar
specialists.

However, this stabilization of Mercaniad will
undoubtedly result in the destabilization of its
humanoid civilization. We have willfully destroyed
an irregular astronomical occurrence upon which
the stability of their culture was based. Under the
circumstances, I had no alternative or option available to me that would have permitted me to save
the *Enterprise* and her crew from certain destruc-
tion. Therefore, I took the responsibility upon
myself to openly and willfully violate the Prime
Directive and General Order Number One, realiz-
ing in advance that any stabilization of this star
would alter the culture and life-style of the humanoid inhabitants of Mercan beyond any possibility of
restitution.

My course of action in the immediate future is
not apparent to me at this time. I have aboard the
Enterprise leaders of two of the three political and
social groups of the Mercan culture: Prime Proctor
Lenos and Technic leader Thallan. It therefore
appears to me that I must attempt to convene and
moderate a meeting between the Guardians, the
Proctorate, and the Technic in hopes of helping
them create for themselves a stable new order on
the planet in the total absence of the major lever
possessed by the Guardians to maintain their position in the culture: the Mystery of the Ordeal, the
Guardian ability to forecast with accuracy the
flare-ups of Mercaniad.

Mercaniad will no longer create the Ordeal
because of *our* actions.

Although I may have saved the *Enterprise* and
her crew, I am forced to ask myself the question:
for what have I saved her?

The Mercan science and technology may certainly be up to the task of providing Lieutenant Commander Scott and the Engineering Division with the necessary support to repair the warp drive unit that's required to permit us to return to the Orion Arm and Federation Territory. But will the Mercans help us? Or will their energies instead have been diverted into a planet-wide civil war because of my actions and decisions?

Chapter Eleven

The door signal on Kirk's cabin sounded.

"Come in," he called.

The door slid open with a swish, revealing Spock's tall silhouette against the passageway lights. Kirk did not get up from where he lay stretched out on his back on his bunk.

"I do not wish to disturb you, Captain."

"Come in, Spock. You aren't disturbing me."

The door slid shut behind the First Officer. "I have some data that needs to be brought to your attention, sir," Spock began. "Your intercom seems to be inoperative."

"I needed a few hours of quiet. I've been thinking, Spock."

The First Officer's right eyebrow went up.

"Don't look so querulous, Spock. Even a star-ship captain needs a few moments of peace and quiet occasionally. And even a star-ship captain can engage in logical thinking. . . ."

"I am well aware of the human need for occasional quiet contemplation. That is one trait shared by both humans and Vulcans," Spock told him. "The ship does not require your immediate attention in standard orbit while we're waiting for the Mercans to discover that the

Ordeal is over. However, I did have two items for your consideration. One: Mercaniad is settling down into a stable Class G0 star as predicted and will attain stable status in approximately eight-point-three hours. It will then probably remain as a stable Class G0 star for nearly a billion years. . . ."

"That means that the Guardians will start to come out of their holes to find out what's going on," Kirk remarked. "And we'll need a plan of action by that time."

"True, Captain. But we are beginning to detect occasional bursts of transporter/traveler radiation on the surface in the vicinity of Celerbitan. The Guardians may be coming out early, having already detected the rapid decrease in stellar intensity."

Kirk sighed and sat up on the edge of his bunk. "Thank you, Spock. That data gives me a time frame within which I'm going to have to work."

But Spock did not step toward the door once he had given his report. "Captain . . . Jim, you haven't been on the Bridge for two watches, which is highly unusual for you under circumstances such as these. I presume that, logically, you're extremely concerned over the possibility of violating General Order Number One in addition to questioning whether or not the Mercans— and the Technic in particular—will fight a civil war instead of permitting us to help them in return for helping us repair the warp drive. Am I correct in my assessment of your predicament?"

Kirk looked up at the tall officer who, with his half-human and half-Vulcan heritage, could often see deep within the thoughts of his human colleagues with an empathy beyond that possible to a human. It wasn't often that Spock permitted himself to address his very close friend James Kirk by his given name, even in private. In this regard, the First Officer's manners were quite Mercan in character. "Sit down, Spock. You've pegged my problem precisely. I may have handled this thing so badly thus far that I don't know if I can carry it through from here . . . even if I forget the Prime Directive entirely and concentrate solely on saving the *Enterprise* and the crew."

Spock didn't answer immediately, but appeared to ponder his captain's words carefully. Then he said, "Jim, we were placed in a highly unusual position by circumstances over which we had no control. You had no alternative but to act in an opportunistic fashion in your handling this totally unique Mercan culture. . . ."

"No, Spock, that's not entirely it," Kirk objected with a wave of his hand. "I should've listened more carefully to you when you warned of the gravitational anomalies near the rift. . . ."

It was obvious that Spock did not accept that premise. "Totally unpredictable. We were operating in uncharted space. . . ."

"Be that as it may, we found the Mercan civilization . . . and I operated with the naive assumption that they were logical, rational humanoids. I was lulled into this by the extreme politeness of Mercan social customs. I didn't act forcefully enough or quickly enough. The Mercans—the Guardians in particular—are no more rational or logical than any other humanoid race . . . even Vulcans," he added guardedly.

"You are correct. Even Vulcans. It requires years to achieve complete control over emotions, even for a Vulcan. Very few Vulcan Masters manage to achieve complete, logical rationality in their thought processes, even after the long and arduous ordeal of the *Kolinahr*," Spock admitted. He hesitated for a moment as though he were highly reluctant to admit a personal matter even to a friend as close as Jim Kirk, the only human whom he could call his *t'hy'la*. "It is my hope that someday I shall be able to return to Vulcan and study under the Masters to achieve this total rationality of logical thought . . . when we get back."

Kirk rose to his feet. "Spock, there you have what I was just in danger of losing: *hope!* Not *if* we get back, but *when* we get back! I was beginning to lose hope!"

"I'm sorry. That's my mother's human heritage making itself visible through me," Spock apologized.

"But I needed to be reminded that it's one of our human strengths," Kirk told him. "I'd run out of options, Spock. I could see only two paths open to me."

Again the right eyebrow of the First Officer went up. "And you believe these to be . . . ?"

Kirk ticked them off on his fingers. "One: because we have such a slim chance of being able to repair the warp drive, I could order the crew to beam down to Mercan, where we might be able to live out the rest of our lives, perhaps working toward the repair of the drive, perhaps just waiting for the Federation star ship that will undoubtedly follow in our track and find this truant star system. Two: I've violated the Prime Directive already, so I could continue on this path and intervene to an even greater degree in what I'm sure is going to turn into a civil war between the Guardians and the Proctors on one side and the Technic on the other. The second option gives us a slim chance to get the warp drive repaired eventually if we back the Technic in the overthrow of the status quo. . . . And we'll win with our advanced weaponry. But the damage, Spock! The damage to the culture of Mercan is a price that even I, a non-Mercan, am not willing to pay!"

Kirk fell silent. Spock continued to look at him in anticipation. When Kirk did not continue, Spock asked, "Why do you think there are only those two options?"

"They're the only ones I can foresee at this moment with the information I have in hand."

"There are more," Spock stated flatly. "As with any consideration of future activities, there's a continually branching decision tree that lies ahead . . . and that decision tree has more than the two stems that you mentioned, Jim."

"Do you have something to add?" Kirk wanted to

know. This was perhaps the longest private conversation Kirk had ever had with the taciturn First Officer.

"I do. There are two items that have been part of our Star Fleet training and education," Spock pointed out. "The first of these is one that I have seen you carry through on many occasions: One does not capitulate until one is absolutely certain that there are no further alternatives. I believe that Lieutenant William Burrows of the old United States Navy, the commanding officer of another USS *Enterprise* in 1813, said, 'The colors must never be struck.' The second is one that I've watched you inculcate into young officers aboard this ship and is just as important: Don't make *any* decision concerning future action until and unless it is absolutely necessary to do so. If you will pardon me for bringing it to your attention, Jim, I detect that you have possibly neglected both. . . ."

Kirk didn't reply for a long moment, then said, "You're right, Spock."

"We were assigned to this mission on a 'rest-and-relaxation' basis," Spock went on quietly. "We were all exhausted when we began . . . and we have not had the time or the circumstances that were anticipated to permit us to come back to the sort of alert duty status of which we are normally capable. In short, Jim, I believe that Doctor McCoy would certainly confirm the fact that you and many other human members of the crew are still fatigued . . . a physical and psychological fact that's had a definite bearing on performance. . . ."

"And you're not exhausted, too?"

"No, I am not. As you know, I am capable of greater endurance than humans."

"Okay, Spock, so much for the McCoy approach . . . although I appreciate that you brought it to my attention. I'm sure I'll get it from McCoy, once Bones can break himself away from Sick Bay," Kirk observed. "What do you believe our options are at this point?"

"Let's consider the facts," Spock said persistently. "No matter what we do from this point, we've already caused irrevocable changes in the Mercan culture and life-style. Therefore, the Prime Directive no longer has any meaning or bearing on this case. It cannot logically be considered as a valid restraint."

"True. Unfortunate, but true."

"Perhaps not unfortunate. That assessment may be premature. It depends on how the Mercans are handled," Spock pointed out. "The second fact is that the Mercans have a well-advanced civilization that's technically competent. In my own judgment, based upon working with Thallan and Othol since they came aboard, I must report to you that they are adaptable, intelligent, and at least as advanced in most respects as nearly every one of the present members of the Federation were at the time they were contacted and joined the Federation."

"I'd sensed that in the Technic people we beamed up," Kirk admitted. "But you haven't tried to deal with the Guardians or the Proctors, Spock. They're as pigheaded and hidebound as any high-priest class or military caste we've ever run into."

"Perhaps. But I have spent some time with Prime Proctor Lenos, too. He was beamed aboard as a very confused man who had his value system completely destroyed by the *Enterprise* and the physical fact that we were *not* from the Abode of Life," Spock pointed out quietly. "He needed help . . . and so did the other members of his Proctor squad who have been in detention since coming aboard. Because of our remote similarity in appearance, he sought me out."

"I can understand that, Spock. We must be like pygmies to them."

"There is more to it than ectomorphism," Spock said. "Their militarism really isn't military at all. It bears faint resemblance to the Romulan philosophy. It's not merely an approach that uses the application of physical force to uphold traditions, rules, codes, and regulations; it's a feeling of duty that you and I would understand, an obligation freely taken to guard, to prevent harm, to rescue and succor in addition to acting on behalf of the Guardians."

Kirk thought for a moment about this, because it triggered a memory deep within him, something that once had been said at Star Fleet Academy during a discussion of paramilitary history. Ah, yes! Lieutenant Robert Henley! "You must remember," the military historian had told him, "that all military, paramilitary or police organizations do not necessarily have to be instruments for the application of physical force to coerce desired action. They can be like the classical model upon which much of Star Fleet is based: the old United States Coast Guard. . . ."

"Then you think we can possibly work with Lenos?" Kirk wanted to know.

"It is quite likely."

This was a new wrinkle in the situation, Kirk realized. Perhaps with the Proctorate teamed with the Technic, the Guardians could be forced to . . . No, that wouldn't work! Kirk wanted them to establish a modified form of the stable culture that they had originally found on Mercan upon their arrival . . . but without the important parareligious factor of the instability of Mercaniad.

"Stability . . . " Kirk muttered.

"Sir?"

"They must work out a system that will give them the same sort of stability they had, Spock."

"Agreed, Captain. Like all humanoids, they are basically a violent race. On Vulcan, we exorcised emotions to overcome our violent nature; the Mercans have ritualized it in their *code duello*. Since the destabilizing factor was external—our accidental arrival here—perhaps an external factor can also be the new stabilizing factor," Spock suggested.

"Membership in the Federation?"

"Precisely, Captain."

"But are they ready for it? The Guardians . . . the Proctorate . . . ?"

"Vulcan was brought into the Federation under similar conditions, Captain," Spock reminded him. "One of the drivers was the desire of both parties for an exchange of valuable information not otherwise obtainable!"

"Spock," Kirk said quietly, "you don't know how much I value our relationship and your logical inputs to my decision-making process. . . ."

"It is my . . . duty, Captain."

"Do you have any recommendations concerning the situation?"

"Captain, I am not qualified in matters of interplanetary diplomacy. . . ."

"Dammit, Spock," Kirk reprimanded him gently, "I'm asking for more of those logical inputs."

Spock didn't reply immediately. Then he said, "Parleys would seem to be in order. A transfer of information is always a helpful start in any negotiation. . . ."

"Ummm . . . Spock, suppose the Guardians won't talk?"

"Then, Captain, you may be reluctantly forced to assume the role of a benevolent dictator. . . ."

"A Hernando Cortes? Forget it, Spock. I couldn't play that role."

"How about a Douglas MacArthur, sir?"

Before Kirk could reply to that, the door signal activated. "Who is it?" Kirk called, obviously irritated at an interruption at this particular moment, when he had established such an unusual and helpful rapport with Spock.

"Doctor McCoy, Captain. Are you all right? Your intercom doesn't answer."

Kirk sighed. "Come in, Bones."

The door sighed open and McCoy entered. As the door slid shut behind him, the Medical Officer saw Spock. "Sorry. Didn't mean to interrupt a conference, gentlemen." Then he peered closely at Kirk. "Are you all right, Jim?"

"Tired, but otherwise functional, Bones. Perturbed

and frustrated, perhaps, by the course of events, but that's part of this job."

"Better come down to Sick Bay and let me check you over for possible side effects of exposure to those hyper-Berthold Rays."

"Has there been a problem with any of the other members of the landing party in that regard, Bones?" Kirk wanted to know.

"Not so far. But I'd like to keep tabs on the four of us."

"Heal yourself first, Bones. We've got some real problems with Mercan," Kirk snapped at his Medical Officer, and was immediately sorry he'd done so.

"Well! Fatigue has caused a bit of irritability—in my medical opinion," McCoy observed.

"Bones, if you came here to check on my welfare, you've got your diagnosis," Kirk told him curtly.

"That was only part of the reason, Jim," the ship's doctor admitted. "I know the social situation with Mercan is bothering you; I saw that down on the planet." He indicated a report board in his right hand. "I've got a great deal of bio data now, thanks to Delin. . . . And, Jim, if Delin is an example of the level of intelligence and technical know-how on Mercan, these people are going to be very effective Federation members. Why, they know some things about bio-engineering we haven't even thought about yet."

"I suspected as much," Spock put in, raising the left eyebrow this time.

"Okay, Bones, brief me. Do you want to do it here or in the Briefing Room?"

"Oh, this will do fine."

"Very well, report."

"Jim, the Mercans are so humanoid that we could interbreed with them," Bones McCoy announced. "Just like the Vulcans."

"I expected that, too," Spock remarked.

"And what logic led you to that conclusion, Spock?" McCoy wanted to know.

"Bones, never mind. If we're that close to the Mercans biologically, do you have any data that might indicate their basic heritage?" Kirk asked. "In other words, were you able to determine from blood analysis where they could have come from?"

"Well, now, blood fractions don't tell the whole story in this case," the doctor went on. "Delin permitted us to perform biopsies on her and allowed us to conduct a complete medical work-up, including internal scans. There's a definite resemblance to Vulcan genetic make-up, in spite of the fact that there's little superficial resemblance in the DNA. When we were down on Mercan, I sensed they were more Vulcan than human, which they are, in spite of subtle differences in genetic and internal structure. So the Mercans are *not* of the basic root stock of humans. In the galactic humanoid matrix, they probably occupy a position between Vulcans and humans, but they're closer to the Vulcan-Romulan group. One thing for certain: the Mercans are going to cause great confusion in xeno-anthropology. I tell you, Jim, this has been as frustrating to me as it's been exciting. With all apologies, Spock, I think the Mercans are probably more like humanized Vulcans."

Spock was nodding.

Kirk noticed it. "Spock, have you come to some conclusions that McCoy and I haven't because of your own background?"

"In a way, Captain. I suspected the possible Vulcan humanoid branch similarity in the Mercans the moment I first beamed down. It was reinforced during my meetings with Prime Proctor Lenos," Spock explained. He paused for a few seconds, then added, "I was able to sense . . . to achieve . . . to accomplish . . . I'm sorry, but you have no concept and therefore no terminology to describe it. There is a Vulcan word, unpronounceable for your speech mechanisms. . . . It doesn't precisely mean 'mind meld,' which you have seen me accomplish. . . . The closest terminology that I can think of to describe it is 'mind touch,' although that is also imprecise."

"Empathy?" McCoy volunteered.

"Something of that sort, Doctor. It's undoubtedly the factor that caused me to suspect the close resemblance to the Vulcan-Romulan humanoid genetic group. . . ."

"All right," Kirk said, beginning to pace back and forth in the cramped space of his quarters, "now I'm beginning to get a handle on how to proceed here. We're going to attempt to parley. But I want our team to consist of myself, Spock, McCoy, and . . . " Kirk thought for a moment. "And Lieutenant Commander Montgomery Scott. We'll speak first with the four members of the Technic that are aboard. Then we'll speak with Lenos and three of the Proctors of his choice from his personal squad that are aboard. Spock, I want you and Doctor McCoy to interface with Lenos and his Proctors initially; I want you to give them a complete tour of the *Enterprise* with as much of an explanation of everything as they are capable of grasping. In particular, I want you to show and explain to them our weaponry and our transporter, Spock."

"Understood, sir."

"I'm going to hold parleys on the *Enterprise* between the four of us and the four Mercans of the Technic and of the Proctorate . . . separately."

"Jim, I know it helps you think, but this pacing back and forth is not only difficult here in your quarters with the two of us present," McCoy interrupted, "but it indicates your nerves are about as taut as a tent rope in the rain. I want you and Scotty to work out together for thirty minutes in the gym . . today! That's a medical order, suh."

Kirk had stopped his pacing. "Very well, Doctor," he snapped, knowing that the ship's doctor was the only person aboard who could give him a direct order relating to physical and mental health. "You're right, I need it."

"So does Scotty," McCoy added.

Kirk pointed at the doctor. "But, Bones, once we've completed those initial parleys aboard, *you're* beaming back to Celerbitan with us as part of the landing party that goes to talk to the Guardians."

"Why me?" McCoy wanted to know. "Damned if I want my molecules scrambled by that transporter again."

"Because *this* time we're beaming down with the full intent of *forcing* the Guardians to parley—and this time I will not hesitate to use force if necessary," Kirk told him firmly. "If the Guardians continue to be stubborn and dogma-bound, there're going to be some fireworks —first from the *Enterprise* up here, then from the landing party on the ground. And considering the damage those Mercan muskets can inflict if one of their bullets ever hits one of us, I want to have a very good medic on hand!"

Chapter Twelve

The regular Briefing Room was not used for any of the meetings with the Mercans. Kirk chose instead to set up a complete briefing and conference room on Deck 11 in the Interconnecting Dorsal of the ship. There was a definite reason for this: the standard lounge on Deck 11 had viewports on both sides of the room through which the outside of the *Enterprise,* the slow march of the planet Mercan beneath the orbiting star ship, and the brilliant glow of the Orion and Sagittarius Arms of the Galaxy or the disc of Mercaniad, could be seen at all times by everyone in the room. The psychological impact was felt even by Kirk the first time he walked in to inspect the facilities before meeting there with the Technic.

Kirk had gotten used to the claustrophilic life to which every star traveler must adapt. Serving aboard a star ship means living in a closed artificial environment with no actual view of the outside universe except as may be provided from time to time by viewscreens. Kirk's duties rarely permitted him to visit the lounge decks in the Interconnecting Dorsal where viewports were provided through which crew members could actually see out of their little artificial world.

So the visual impact of actually *seeing* Mercan and

the glittering bands of light of the Galactic Arms was almost overwhelming, even to him. He stepped out of the turbolift and walked to the port side, where he stood for a long moment, watching the blue, white, green, and brown surface of the Abode of Life slide past. He turned to find Scotty at his side.

"Captain," the Engineering Officer said softly in a highly unusual expression of Gaelic emotion, "sometimes I dinna think we take enough time to smell the flowers as we go tearin' around the Galaxy. . . ."

If the setting had *that* sort of impact on Lieutenant Commander Montgomery Scott, who usually saw beauty in nothing except engineering drawings and operational manuals, Kirk knew that this was the proper site for the discussions with the Mercans. . . .

If only he could now manage to get Pallar and the other Guardians up here to see this without using force to do so!

Insofar as Kirk was concerned, there was no question about it: he had to *force* them to come here if necessary. If the Guardians persisted in acting like stubborn children, Kirk had resigned himself to the fact that he would have to rub their noses in it . . . hard.

He thought he knew what the reaction of the Technic people would be, but had serious doubts as to how Lenos and his Proctors would behave. However, Kirk underestimated the psychological impact in both instances.

When Thallan, Delin, Othol, and Orun stepped off the turbolift onto the Deck 11 lounge, all four of them stopped dead in their tracks at the sight of the universe beyond the viewports on both sides.

Kirk stepped forward to welcome Thallan, but found that the Technic leader was utterly stunned by the sight. The elderly Mercan merely looked from side to side, trying to fit what he was seeing into his own concepts.

"Welcome, Thallan. There is your Abode of Life," Kirk told him.

In spite of what was now an extensive exposure to the Mercan language, none of the people aboard the *Enterprise* had really learned how to speak it, and Translators were still used . . . although everyone was getting used to them by now and hardly noticed them except when the devices failed to make a translation and uttered the equivalent of a stammer.

This was the case with Kirk's Translator when Thallan gave vent to an emotional quasi-religious phrase in the Mercan language that simply would not translate. Yet, from Thallan's tone of voice, Kirk knew that the Technic leader was emotionally stirred. He finally pulled himself together to the point where he said to Kirk, "I have spent my life on the Abode, working to justify the belief that there was more to the universe and to life than just the Abode. . . . I was elated when we traveled to the *Enterprise,* but it was just like working in the windowless Keeps. Even the viewscreens you have did not give me the feeling that I'm getting now. Here I am facing the reality of what I've mentally believed all my life . . . and it's almost too much for me to accept."

Kirk had timed the meeting carefully. As the Mercans stood there in awe of the sight before them, the white-bright disc of Mercaniad touched the curved horizon of Mercan, slipped below the planet's limb, and splayed bands of color in both directions through the Mercanian atmosphere. As quickly as it happened, it was gone.

And the brilliant bands of the Orion and Sagittarius Arms of the Galaxy became visible, brighter than the Mercans had ever seen them before, now that there was no atmosphere to attenuate the light.

"Thallan, why didn't you tell us it could be so beautiful?" Delin wanted to know.

"Because one cannot truly describe beauty that one has never experienced. . . ."

Othol was at the starboard viewports, looking out at the galactic arms. "There is where we came from. And,

THE ABODE OF LIFE 155

Kirk, you say those are uncountable numbers of suns like Mercaniad?"

"Some of them are bigger than a hundred Mercaniads," Spock pointed out.

Thallan shook his head. He indicated the three young Mercans. "They will have an easier time adjusting to these new realities than I, even though I have thought about them for longer than they have lived."

"Honored guests of the United Federation of Planets," Kirk said, the Translator sounding out the full syllables of the formal, stilted-sounding Mercan language in response to Kirk's use of the full formal Federation language of diplomacy. "Please sit down so that we may talk. I've asked Mister Spock, Mister Scott, and Doctor McCoy to join me so that your group and my group may be of equal size and importance. Yeoman Janice Rand won't take part in our discussions but will make a record of them for the mutual use of both our groups, should we wish to refer later to some matter we have discussed. Is this arrangement satisfactory to you?"

Kirk had deliberately elimated the usual conference table because in the entire time he had spent on the Abode, he'd never once seen the Mercans sit around a table. When he and the rest of the landing party had been grilled by Pallar and the Guardians, there'd been no table. Kirk knew why. Everyone was armed . . . including the four Star Fleet officers and Yeoman Janice Rand, all carrying Mark II hand phasers in full view. In addition, Kirk wore the Mercan sidearm that Orun had purchased for him in Celerbitan. Armed citizens operating under a *code duello* could not confer in an environment where part of them was hidden as it would be if seated around a table. Only Yeoman Rand was seated with a small desk beside her on the aft side of the deck. Nor could Kirk assume that firearms would be placed upon the table; he assumed that a sidearm in a holster was the only acceptable place for it to be when it wasn't in social use by the Mercans. He was right.

"Would you care for refreshment?" Kirk asked after they had seated themselves in a semicircle of seats facing one another.

Thallan declined. "We assume you have asked us to meet with you so that we may discuss the new situation on the Abode created by your arrival here and your subsequent stabilization of Mercaniad."

"Partly," Kirk replied.

"I'm not certain that the four of us are authorized or qualified to speak for or on behalf of the Technic group in matters involving the future course of events on the Abode," Thallan pointed out.

"Would you wish to return to the Abode at your convenience to discuss matters with your Technic Peers?" Kirk asked. He was willing to do that for any of the three groups, but he was not about to let them go back down without an escort from the *Enterprise:* a group of selected security people. "We can arrange that easily. But for now, we would speak with you as temporary representatives of the Technic Peers. We also intend to speak privately with a group from the Proctorate as well as with a group of Guardians *here* in this room where they can see what everyone else has seen. We'll then bring all three groups here to meet together concerning your future political arrangement on the Abode while we of the United Federation of Planets sit by to advise you concerning the Federation, should you care to apply for membership."

"You intend to bring these three Mercan groups together?"

"We do. And we will not interfere with the deliberations that must take place between them."

"You don't intend to side with the Technic in bringing about the new order of things on Mercan?" Othol asked incredulously.

"We don't live on the Abode. It's your problem that you must solve yourselves," Kirk explained. "Under the provisions of our own code, we can't intervene in your affairs on the Abode."

"But—" Othol began.

"But," Kirk broke in, "we can assist you by showing you, the Proctorate, and the Guardians how similar problems of living together have been solved on other abodes. That's one reason why I asked you to meet with us now. When the Proctorate and the Guardians each meet privately with us, they'll be told and shown the same things that we'll tell and show you. But how we tell and show you things will depend upon your answer to this simple question: Do you now believe that we came from the Ribbon of Night out *there"*— Kirk indicated the glowing spiral galactic arms outside the starboard viewports—"and that there might be other abodes similar to yours there as well?"

"Yes." All four Mercan Technics answered together without hesitation.

"Good. That makes our job easier," Kirk replied. "Each of us has worked with the library computer of the *Enterprise* to assemble a visual presentation of the Universe as we now believe it to be, accompanied by a brief description of life on some of the abodes of the Federation and an outline of our individual specialized fields of knowledge. I'll discuss the Federation and its history. Mister Spock will give you a brief rundown on the general level of scientific knowledge. Doctor McCoy will discuss our medical technology as well as the life forms of some of the abodes. And Mister Scott will talk about our technology, engineering, and the star ship *Enterprise*. But this is not a unilateral meeting. Once we have told you about *us,* we want you to tell us about yourselves, about Mercan, about the Technic, and about *your* knowledge. Everything that we do together must always be a mutual exchange, and the first thing that we must exchange in order to achieve later agreement is information about one another. Is this agreed?"

Thallan looked upon the dark surface of his world below, then out at the galactic arms thrown across the black sky of space. "I didn't expect that you, with all your power and weaponry, which far exceeds ours, would meet us on an equal level. Our own history is not devoid of stories of conflicts and conquests of the stronger over the weaker before the days of the Code of the Abode when the contests were brought down to the level of individual confrontations. James Kirk, you of the Federation are not only stranger than we originally thought you must be, but stranger than we ever thought possible."

"You're not describing just the Federation, Thallan. That's the way we look upon the entire Universe!"

Captain's Log: Stardate 5079.3

The plan of the meetings that was thrashed out between Mister Spock, Doctor McCoy, Mister Scott, and I may work after all. I'm very encouraged after our meeting with the four Mercan Technics . . . but I have to keep reminding myself that this is the easiest of the three Mercan groups we're going to meet. The Technic group will most certainly make my job easier, even though they're initially opposed to granting any position to the Guardians in the new arrangement; the Technic people aboard believe that the Guardians' role is no longer required and that the Technic can now assume that mantle of semipriesthood. But Thallan and the rest have to mull over what they saw and heard during the meeting . . . and they're *not* stupid people. They all took copious notes during our presentations, writing furiously in that script of theirs that appears so much like Arabic. Thallan wants to return to the surface, but I don't want to let any of them off the ship until we've met with the Guardians . . . which are going to be the toughest of the three groups to work with.

I'm trying very hard *not* to play the conquistador role by leading these people in any direction.

They've *got* to work out their differences themselves. None of us aboard knows enough about the
Mercan civilization yet to force a viable arrangement on them that would work, much less endure
long enough to prevent a planetary civil war. The
only thing I insist I must do is to keep hammering
away at them, if necessary, to compromise and
come to an agreement. That is why these meetings
will take place here aboard the *Enterprise,* where
one disenchanted or stubborn faction can't go
storming out of the conference to whip up that civil
war. I won't let them off the ship to do it. I *must*
make this work . . . or it will be a long time before
Star Fleet has the opportunity to listen to this. . . .

Kirk didn't meet Prime Proctor Lenos and three of
his Proctors on Deck 11, as he had the Technic group.
He showed up with Spock, Scotty, and McCoy in the
staterooms where the Proctors were being kept in
security detention. Basically, Kirk didn't want to take
any chances with the chief paramilitary person of the
Abode, although he knew that he'd be required to
follow protocol. Therefore, the Federation group
would accompany the Proctors from their detention
staterooms along a well-planned route to Deck 11 with
ship security personnel stationed inconspicuously along
the route . . . all armed with phasers set for stun. The
Federation group wore full dress uniforms, and both
Kirk and Scotty carried their Mercan sidearms in
addition to hand phasers in full view, Scotty draping his
baldric over his shoulder and kilt.

"Proctor Lenos," Kirk announced as they entered
the Prime Proctor's stateroom, "the four of us from the
United Federation of Planets would be honored to have
you and three of your chosen Proctors accompany us to
a place where we may talk as equals concerning the
future of the Abode. This will be a peaceful exchange
of information between equals. As such, we'll return

your weapons to you for the meeting so that we may indeed be equals. But our code does not match your code, and I must tell you that we'll permit no violence on the part of the Proctor group. Will you agree to meet under those terms?" Kirk extended Lenos' long-barreled Proctorate repeating firearm butt-first toward the Prime Proctor.

Lenos looked the Federation group over carefully, noting that each was armed, some properly with Mercan weapons, and all with the strange but powerful weapons he did not understand. He also noted that they'd dressed differently than he'd seen them before; their clothing bore more ornaments and sigils of rank and was therefore obviously attire worn when conferring with those of extremely high position such as himself. He stood up, reached for his armored helmet, placed it upon his head, and reached for the weapon that Kirk extended toward him. "It is agreed. I would prefer to talk and exchange information than to sit in this room doing nothing. There is much that we must talk about, and much that I would like to know."

"There may be more to know than you're aware of, Prime Proctor," Kirk told him, releasing the weapon to him.

It was an unusual parade that strode through the corridors and passageways of the *Enterprise* to the turbolift—a column of twos with each Proctor being accompanied by one of the Federation parley group. The security forces were not in evidence.

When the turbolift door swished open on the Deck 11 meeting room and Kirk stepped out with Lenos at his side, the Prime Proctor marched ten steps into the room . . . and stopped. Fortunately, this was far enough into the room to permit the others to clear the turbolift.

Mercaniad shone through the starboard viewports, which had been polarized to cut down the glare.

On the port view, the Proctors could look down and see the island of Celerbitan passing beneath the orbiting star ship. There would be no question in the mind of any Mercan that this was Celerbitan, for all who used the traveler would have learned the geography of the Abode through the Traveler Directory. Again, Kirk's planning group had thought through every detail of each separate meeting, and this one was timed to provide the proper impact for the Proctors.

It overimpacted Lenos.

He slowly removed his helmet, muttering something in a voice so low that the Translators couldn't pick it up. His helmet suddenly clattered to the deck and he became ramrod-stiff, staring out the viewports toward his home planet for the first time, seeing and yet not wanting to see.

Spock, who was right behind him, saw what had happened to the Prime Proctor. "Severe psycho-trauma," the Vulcan First Officer observed, and stepped around in front of Lenos.

He was quickly joined by McCoy, who looked at the Prime Proctor and said, "He's probably on the edge of catatonia, Spock."

Spock nodded, then placed his right hand over the Prime Proctor's face. His own face showed strain as he closed his eyes.

"Spock, no! You've never tried mind meld with a Mercan before!" Kirk objected. "They're close enough to you that you could—"

"Captain, Spock must try," McCoy replied, because Spock was totally concentrating on Lenos. "The Mercan's gone into traumatic psycho-shock. He can't permit himself to believe what he's seeing, because his Proctorate training won't allow it. Spock must break through that . . . or you'll never be able to confer with *any* Proctor up here."

A low moan came from Spock, who then began to mumble Vulcan and Mercan words. Finally he groaned, "Yes . . . yes. . . . It is not all wrong. . . . It is only part of what is true. . . . The Abode is real. . . . You are real. . . . This is real. . . ." He gave an almost explosive exhalation of breath, then opened his eyes and removed his hand from Lenos' forehead.

Lenos' eyes snapped open and he looked directly at Spock. "You have been very helpful, and I will not forget it, Spock."

Spock turned his head to Kirk and explained quietly, "A Proctor cannot permit himself to faint. . . ."

The other three Proctors did not go into the same degree of psycho-shock as Lenos, but one would not expect that from other than a Proctor who had exhibited the discipline and mental rigidity to rise to the very top of such a paramilitary organization. However, McCoy and Spock spoke to each of them quietly, more to assure themselves that there was no problem than to offer the sort of therapy that Spock had conducted with Lenos.

When the eight sat down together, Kirk realized that this would be a meeting of paramilitary men rather than a meeting of scientists, as with the Technic group. It was fortunate for Kirk that he was a star-ship captain.

"We're meeting here," Kirk announced, "so that you might see for yourselves that I spoke the truth when I said we did not come from the Abode but traveled in a small world from the Ribbon of Night."

"James Kirk," Prime Proctor Lenos said with exaggerated lack of emotion that was betrayed only by his eyes, "I could not believe you then because what I'd been taught to believe could not be expanded to include the truth of what you said. Now I see the Abode on one side and Mercaniad on the other . . . and I know for the first time that we're not on the Abode. I accept this as reality. I must therefore also accept the other things that you've said, even though they may conflict with what I have known to be truth. . . ."

"Prime Proctor," Kirk replied with equal lack of emotion and curtness, "we don't require that you or any Mercan change your belief in the Code. However, the reality of the Universe will require you to add new information to the Code . . . which will not really change the Code very much at all."

"Why do you wish to show us these things and to talk with us?" Lenos wanted to know. "With your power, your weapons, and your traveling world, will you be displacing the Guardians by force and require the Proctorate . . . or do you wish to discuss an arrangement with us for participation in the conflict in exchange for our services thereafter?"

"Neither. We meet because there are changes that you must understand," Kirk tried to explain. "The role of the Proctorate need not be changed drastically if suitable agreements can be reached between the Technic, the Guardians, and the Proctorate."

"I find it difficult to believe that you don't intend to conquer and rule," Lenos said bluntly. "We haven't had conflict and conquest on the Abode for uncounted generations, but we have stories from the time before the Code, when such things occurred. You have the capability for conquest. We would fight, but we might not win. With my background and training, I must tell you that we haven't fought for so long that it would be difficult for us at first . . . then difficult for you later, even with your capability."

Kirk said slowly and carefully, "We don't choose to use our capability for conquest except to prevent conflict between Mercans because of the change." There were times when the formal and stilted language usage of Mercan had its advantages, and this was one of them.

"What is this change you speak of?"

"Mercaniad will no longer create an Ordeal. To save ourselves, we were forced to tamper with Mercaniad to stabilize it. There will be no further need for the Guardian Mysteries of the Ordeal. There will be no further need for the Keeps. There would be no need for change if only the Guardians and the Proctorate knew this, but the Technic knows it, too . . . and all Mercans will know it soon," Kirk explained. "We're speaking of this separately to the Technic, to the Guardians, and to you, the Proctorate. Then we'll bring all three groups to the *Enterprise* so that together you may discuss and work out solutions for the change without having to resort to conflict."

"You'd speak of this with the Technic?" Lenos asked indignantly.

"We've done so because they *knew* of the change of Mercaniad."

"An open conflict with the Technic would pose no problem for the Proctorate," Lenos boasted.

"So? You just told me that you hadn't fought for many generations. Thallan of the Technic has told us that the Technic is capable of building and using weapons superior to yours; they haven't fought, either, so you're on equal ground there. But they may have superior weapons. Do you wish to risk losing to them? Or would you be willing to talk about an arrangement first?" Kirk paused for a moment and added, "Lenos, I *have* fought. I tell you in truth that I'd rather come to an agreement by talking than to fight. I've seen my friends killed; I've seen my enemies die. It doesn't produce personal satisfaction for a paramilitary person such as you or me to fight. As Captain of the *Enterprise,* I'm trained to fight if absolutely necessary . . . but only if there's no other recourse! Am I correct in saying that your Proctorate training is the same?"

Lenos thought about this for a long moment during which he watched impassively as Mercaniad slipped behind the edge of the Abode and the Ribbon of Night became visible. Then he said, "Captain James Kirk, at first you were strange and different. Now I see that you and your people only appear to be different. We think alike in many ways. I believe that we may be able to work together to accomplish our real duty which is the prevention of conflict. Please tell me what you recommend the first joint action should be. . . ."

Kirk smiled. He'd won two out of three now. "Prime

Proctor, I suspect we've both been taught that the first action to take in any operation is to obtain and evaluate information upon which future action may be soundly based. Is this correct?"

The Prime Proctor of the Abode of Life inclined his head upward in the Mercan gesture of affirmation.

"Then let us first exchange information about one another so that we may work together more soundly toward the goal of stabilizing and expanding the Code of the Abode."

Chapter Thirteen

Captain's Log: Stardate 5080.7

In a few minutes, I'll beam down with a landing party to the island-city of Celerbitan and the Guardian Villa on the surface of Mercan, the Abode of Life. This is probably the most critical phase of our attempt to stabilize the civilization of Mercan.

Our meeting with the Technic group led by Thallan revealed that their technology is well-advanced due to the copious amounts of iron, aluminum, and copper available on or near the surface of the planet, with high-quality lodes deep in the mantle, where the Mercans built their Keeps generations ago. These lodes and ore bodies have been relatively undisturbed because, without a large moon and tidal strains, Mercan is a tectonically stable planet with little movement of its continental plates. Thus, it's been easy for the Mercans to develop the iron-based technology we find on nearly all Type M planets inhabited by humanoids.

Although the Mercans seem to have forgotten a lot of the older technology that preceded the universal use of their traveler system, my Engineering Officer believes that the Technic possesses the necessary technology in metallurgy, materials science, and antimatter know-how to provide us with raw materials and finished parts built to Scott's specifications, even though the Mercans don't have antimatter warp drives yet. We shouldn't expect that they'd direct their technology toward star flight anyway. They've developed antimatter as a compact power source for their traveler system.

In the course of talking with the Technic members, we learned that Mercan is also rich in the basic material for an antimatter energy system. The Mercans call it "vitaliar," but Scott says it's an alloy of several elements of the matter-antimatter system. There are also some low-quality dilithium crystals on the planet, but the Mercans never thought to use them in their antimatter systems because they had developed different but more complex techniques. The use of the Mercan dilithium crystals in our systems would not produce the efficiencies we require . . . but there're a lot of these low-quality dilithium crystals on Mercan if we wish to make some modifications to use them. Scott's looking into this now as an alternative if we need additional dilithium crystals for our return journey.

We *might* be able to effect repairs here without the Guardians and without establishing a restabilized civilization on Mercan. But we'd save ourselves and leave a shambles behind. With the technology possessed by the Mercans, there might be nothing left when we got back . . . and I'm sure the Federation will want to establish diplomatic relations, if not offer outright Federation membership to these people. Mercan is in a critical location to support future Federation exploration and colonization of our treaty-permitted sector of the Galaxy in the Sagittarius Arm. In addition, it has valuable ore deposits; even the low-grade dilithium crystals are of value to commercial star ships that don't operate at the high warp speeds of Star Fleet vessels.

Eventually, perhaps in less than a century, the Klingons are likely to work their way this far toward the center of the Galaxy. If we don't have Mercan in the Federation, I know the Klingons would indeed play the conquistador role . . . if they left anything at all except their own fleet base here.

I want to put my thoughts on record before beaming down, because this is a critical operation and I want a record to remain, should something happen.

But we're going down in force this time. Lieutenant Commander Scott will have the conn in my absence. My landing force will consist of Mister Spock, Doctor McCoy, Lieutenant Sulu, and seven of our most experienced security officers under Sulu's command. I intend to convince Pallar and the Guardians to beam up willingly to meet in the ship. If they won't agree to parley in the *Enterprise,* I have Prime Proctor Lenos as a hostage if I wish to use him as such. I'd rather not, since he appears to understand the situation now and is willing to confer, however reluctantly, with the Technic and the Guardians. If Pallar abandons Lenos, we'll get Pallar up here by force. We may have to stun a few Proctors or even some Guardians to do it.

At this point, I'm not averse to using coercion in the form of physical force to bring the Guardians to conference. We've got too much to lose. . . .

In an unusual move, Kirk inspected the landing force before beaming down, wanting to make absolutely sure of every detail because of the critical nature of this mission.

"Spock, I want you to carry your hand phaser in the open where it'll be visible," Kirk told his First Officer, noting that Spock had apparently placed the Mark II phaser under his tunic, where it would normally be carried.

"Captain, a Vulcan never appears in public visibly armed with a weapon except in *Kal-if-fee*," Spock objected.

"On Mercan, you must appear visibly armed," Kirk ordered. "In the Mercan culture, if you're not visibly armed, you're a nobody."

"At your request, Captain, I will follow the local custom," Spock replied.

"Are you sure I really have to wear this again?" McCoy indicated his Mercan sidearm. "I certainly don't intend to use it."

"Wear it, Bones. It's your option to use it or not. You're the medic on this mission. Even though medics don't want to fight, sometimes they have to."

Kirk stepped up on the transporter stage to look over his landing force. "I'll repeat the general order for this mission, gentlemen: if you have to shoot, shoot to stun and not to kill, regardless of what the Mercans do if a fight breaks out. I don't feel it's necessary to repeat any of our recent briefing unless any of you have questions. If you don't understand something, ask now and not on Mercan, where we've got to act in a unified manner. So, for the last time, any questions?"

There were none.

Kirk stepped into a transporter locus and quietly said, "Landing force, prepare to beam down. Places, please."

Then, as everyone stood at the ready, Kirk gave the command, "Energize."

Kirk had selected the spot where they had materialized in the Guardian Villa with Lenos and Orun those many days ago.

There was no one in sight.

"Follow me," Kirk snapped. "Security, cover our rear and check each alcove as we pass it." He strode toward the corridor where he had seen Pallar appear during their first encounter. It ended in a heavy set of double doors. Kirk merely pushed one open and went through.

And found himself face to face with a seated circle of about two dozen Guardians, apparently in conference session.

He strode into the chamber far enough to permit the rest of his landing force to get through the door behind him and array themselves on either side of him.

Pallar rose to greet him. "James Kirk, welcome. We thought you'd perished in the recent Ordeal along with Proctor Lenos and his group."

Following Mercan custom, Kirk replied, "Greetings, Pallar. We're all alive and well, thank you. You may be pleased to learn that Prime Proctor Lenos and his group of Proctors, as well as Thallan, Orun, Delin, and Othol, are alive and well, too."

"You were able to overcome the Proctors and find the safety of a Keep?" Pallar asked incredulously.

"Yes and no," Kirk told him. He still carried his phaser in his hand, as did the rest of his landing force. But the familiar Mercan sidearm was holstered at his side. "Our Keep is in the sky . . . in the traveling device we used to journey here from the Ribbon of Night. Your Prime Proctor and the Technic group are there."

Guardian Noal, seated at Pallar's right, was looking over the landing force carefully. He sneered. "Pallar, he is still insane, as before. These biological constructs of the Technic are obviously able to withstand the Ordeal . . . but I'm truly surprised at the variety of form that the Technic has been able to achieve. Consider the one with the pointed ears. . . ."

"Pallar . . . Guardians . . . we didn't come here to argue the reality of our source with you," Kirk said firmly. "A great change has come over Mercaniad, and this change will create drastic and sweeping changes in your civilization here on the Abode."

"What do you know of Mercaniad?" Guardian Parna asked, rising to her feet.

"Ah, you've noticed?" Kirk asked the rhetorical question with a smile. "Mister Spock here, a citizen of an abode called Vulcan, will be happy to explain it to you."

Spock looked directly at the Guardian council and said in his usual emotionless tone, "Mercaniad has been stabilized. I calculated that the placement of high-energy antimatter explosives we call photon torpedoes in the core of Mercaniad would damp the irregular oscillations in its stellar output. Therefore, I caused those two photon torpedoes to be injected into Mercaniad. Your sun is stabilized. There will be no more Ordeals."

"How have you of the Technic been able to do this and to determine this outcome?" Parna asked directly.

"We aren't of the Technic," Kirk told her, "but Spock knows stellar physics. Mister Spock . . ."

"Your Mystery of Mercaniad is no mystery to those of us in the Star Fleet of the United Federation of Planets," Spock explained carefully. "Your ancestors learned how to measure the critical parameters such as neutrino flux and gravito-inertial radiation, both of which emanate from the stellar core. I am certain that those instruments left to you by your ancestor Guardians will now show that there is minimal variation in these parameters. . . ."

"The Technic has learned the Mysteries of Mercaniad," Guardian Tombah growled.

"We aren't of the Technic," Kirk repeated. "But the Technic knows of this already. However, it doesn't make any difference. With Mercaniad stabilized, the Mysteries of Mercaniad no longer have any validity."

"Pallar, I warned you!" Guardian Aldys shouted at the Guardian One. "We should have had the Proctor-

ate move against the Technic earlier, before they
learned. Now it is too late!"

"The Technic didn't learn any of this from their own
experiments," Kirk tried to point out. "They learned
from us."

"The general populace doesn't know of this yet,"
Pallar pointed out to his colleagues. "There are only a
few who know. Aldys, you and Parna were very
effective in explaining why the recent Ordeal was so
short. So the citizens of Mercan still believe in us.
Therefore, fellow Guardians of the Principle Council, I
submit to you that there is only one thing that we can
do at this point. Do you agree?"

"Kill them!" Noal shouted.

"Destroy them before they can inform," Aldys put
in.

"Proctors!" Tombah yelled.

Three doors to the chamber flew open to reveal
Proctors in their openings.

Kirk was the first to fire. But the concentrated phaser
fire of the lightning-fast security people dropped the
other Proctors almost simultaneously.

The Guardian Johon, seeing this, reacted instinctive-
ly by going for his Mercan sidearm. Spock dropped him
instantly with a stun bolt from his hand phaser.

"Hold!" Kirk shouted above what could become a
melee as he reset the output of his phaser. With cool
aim, he fired a phaser bolt into the floor in front of
Pallar. The floor grew hot, then blew up in an explosion
of shards driven by the vaporization of the latent water
in the flooring.

That stopped the confusion.

"We didn't come here to argue with you and your
Guardians, Pallar," Kirk stated flatly. "We possess
more weapon power than you can possibly imagine!
This has been only an example of it. The Proctors and
Guardian Johon are unhurt; they'll regain conscious-
ness shortly. All the Proctors on the Abode cannot

possibly stop us, because this time we've come in force to show you the truth of that fact."

Pallar stared at Kirk for a moment, then at each member of the landing force. "What do you want of us?" he finally asked.

Another Proctor appeared in an open doorway to the chamber, and the landing force from the *Enterprise* heard a sound few of them had ever experienced. The Proctor fired as he had been trained to do: the first shot went over their heads. The explosion of the Proctor's firearm was followed by the slap sound of the bullet's shock wave as it passed centimeters over their heads. The Proctor was immediately stunned to unconsciousness by a phaser bolt from one of Kirk's security men.

"First of all, call off the Proctors before we become angry and somebody gets hurt," Kirk snapped with obvious irritation in his tone.

As four more Proctors appeared in the doorways, Pallar held up his hand to them. "Cease, Proctors! Secure your weapons!" the Guardian One ordered. "Now, again, James Kirk, what do you want of us?"

"You and three of your Guardians. You may choose who accompanies you," Kirk explained. "We'll travel to our Keep in the sky for a meeting between us, conducted in peace. Then, you'll meet with an equal number of representatives from the Proctorate and the Technic in our Keep for the purpose of working out between your groups a stable social situation here on the Abode."

"We have a stable situation," Guardian Jona remarked.

"Not any longer," Kirk pointed out.

"Guardian Pallar, this is one of the most elaborate and insane plots I have ever encountered," Noal complained. "These Technic constructs are not sane."

"I presume that you're a medical expert, Guardian Noal?" Kirk asked.

"I am."

"Permit me to introduce my medical expert, Doctor Leonard McCoy." Kirk indicated the ship's doctor.

"If you're wondering whether or not we're Technic constructs," McCoy said slowly, "I can easily show you data on blood chemistry alone that proves beyond a doubt that the Technic couldn't possibly possess the technology to create us. You're familiar with blood-chemistry technology?"

"Of course. That's one of the most primitive of medical technologies," Noal replied in an insulted tone.

"Of course. No insult intended, Guardian, so please stay away from your sidearm," McCoy went on. "I'm a medical man, not a warrior. You may kill according to your Code when you have to, but I don't follow that sort of a code. But let me give you some basic data. Your blood chemistry is based on a hemoglobin molecule arranged around an atom of copper. Well, the hemoglobin of Mister Spock here from the abode called Vulcan is also based on copper. But the rest of us have a hemoglobin molecule based on iron. There're other differences in the blood groups, but the hemoglobin fraction is the easiest to check if you have any question about it."

There was a moment of hesitation on Noal's part before he replied, "I would like to look at your data, Doctor McCoy . . . and perhaps I might want to take some blood samples myself. Technic biological know-how may be more highly advanced than we know."

"It isn't," McCoy added with finality. "But mine is. Come see for yourself."

"And we're ready to prove to the rest of you that we are who we say we are," Kirk broke in, moving quickly into the sudden opening in the Guardians' stubborn beliefs created by their medical expert's condescension. "We have the power to simply step in here and take over by force, but that's not our code. We want to repair our abode and return to our people in the

Ribbon of Night. But *you* are the ones who are going to have to continue to live on the Abode, and *you* are the ones who are going to have to solve your own problems your own way. We are here to help you if you want help. Or you can try to solve your problems without what help we're permitted to give you. But you *must* solve those problems or your civilization is going to come apart very quickly without the unifying factor of the Ordeal. Since our arrival here by accident started this whole affair, and since we had to stabilize Mercaniad to save ourselves, we want to see to it that our actions do not totally destroy your civilization. Therefore, we want you to meet on the *Enterprise* to work out the details of the transition to your new state of affairs . . . which is now quite different than you have ever dreamed possible. . . ."

"You want us to confer in your Keep in the sky? Ridiculous!" Tombah laughed.

"Spock, how's our timing?" Kirk wanted to know.

"Overhead in two minutes thirty-four seconds, Captain."

"Have them stand by the phasers," Kirk ordered, then turned back to Pallar. "Come with us out into the open. We'll show you our Keep in the sky as it passes overhead."

The Guardian group looked at one another.

"Well, come along," Kirk urged. "Or are you afraid I might be right? Are you afraid to face the reality of the Universe? Or do you intend to continue living in a fantasy? You don't have to leave the Guardian Villa to see for yourselves. Come anywhere outside where you can see the sky."

"This is most unusual," Guardian Parna objected. "I know what's in the sky. It's now after sunset, and we'll see nothing but the Ribbon of Night."

"I can promise you more," Kirk put in. "Come along and see for yourself."

Some of the Guardians came with more reluctance than others. But Pallar led the way at Kirk's side.

The high hill of the Guardian Villa overlooked the island of Celerbitan and the western skies of Mercan. Mercaniad had just set, and there was a glow across the entire western horizon.

"Enterprise, this is Kirk," the star-ship Captain spoke into the communicator he flipped up in front of his face.

There was a look of astonishment on Pallar's face as Scotty's voice came back, "Scott here, Captain. We're comin' over your horizon now."

"Okay, Scotty, light her up," Kirk ordered, and turned to Sulu. "Mister Sulu, take over."

Sulu flipped out his communicator. *"Enterprise,* this is Sulu. Chekov, are you standing by?"

"Affirmative, Sulu," Chekov's voice replied. "We are tracking the targets that you defined."

"Continue tracking. Stand by for further commands," Sulu told him, but did not close his communicator.

Kirk was looking at the western sky and finally saw it.

It was a brilliant, coruscating point of light. Scotty was illuminating the lower surface of the primary hull with laser light at various frequencies, bouncing the laser illumination off the ship's lower shields to prevent loss of coherency. It made the *Enterprise* shine and coruscate with the characteristic corpuscular appearance of laser illumination and with the brilliance of a minus-five-magnitude star. It changed colors as Scotty changed the frequency of the laser illumination.

"There's our sky Keep, Guardians," Kirk pointed out.

It was impossible not to see it.

There were gasps from some of the Guardians. The sight was totally new to all of them. Some of them obviously grasped and accepted it. Others were obviously having trouble doing so.

"We have power aboard our Keep, the *Enterprise,* that's greater than anything you have known," Kirk said almost pontifically to the Guardian group. "And we'll now prove it to you. Mister Sulu, you may proceed with the demonstration."

As the colored light that was the *Enterprise* rose toward the zenith, Sulu softly gave an order into his communicator. "Chekov, this is Sulu. Set both forward laser banks at broad dispersion, phase lock, and fire a ten-second burst at the ionosphere."

A glow emanated from the spot of light in the sky. Then the whole evening sky lit up as the phasers of the *Enterprise* excited the ionosphere over Celerbitan, producing a brilliant aurora that laced the blackness with streamers of orange and yellow light, spreading from the point of light of the *Enterprise* poleward in both directions.

It was a brilliant display of scientific fireworks. It had been used before to impress more primitive peoples than the Mercans. Kirk was counting on it to impress the Guardians in a different way, since they were considerably above the primitive level in intelligence and civilization.

Then came the *pièce de résistance*. "Port and starboard phaser banks, tight beam, phase lock, target the ocean five kilometers west of Celerbitan, two-second burst. Fire at will," Sulu ordered.

Twin beams of incredibly white light emanated from the *Enterprise* and speared through the Mercan atmosphere, ionizing a pathway as they penetrated. They focused and struck the Sel Ethan ocean five kilometers off the west shore of Celerbitan, where the water suddenly boiled. It didn't last long—only two seconds —but it was enough to boil a square kilometer of ocean and leave a rising cloud of steam.

As the Guardians gaped at this obvious and blatant display of star-ship weapon power, Kirk said to Pallar, "That's the *Enterprise,* our Keep in the sky. Prime Proctor Lenos is there. So are Thallan, Orun, Delin, and Othol. We invite you to select three of your Guardians and travel with us to the *Enterprise* for discussions."

"How do I know that this isn't a trick to eliminate us?" Pallar asked. "You've demonstrated weaponry that could conquer the Abode, causing a conflict and conquest like those in the old legends."

"Conquest is not part of our code," Kirk explained, then pointed out, "And if we'd wanted to destroy you rather than to talk, we could have done so at any time since we arrived here . . . and with great ease, as you just saw." He displayed his communicator. "You originally believed this to be a sigil of rank. It's more than that. It permits us to talk with those on the *Enterprise*." He spoke into it. "*Enterprise,* this is Kirk. Lieutenant Uhura, please put Prime Proctor Lenos on."

"Uh . . . Captain Kirk, this is the Prime Proctor," came back a voice that was unquestionably that of Lenos. It was also obvious that he was unused to any remote-communication device.

Kirk handed the communicator to Pallar. "Speak to your Prime Proctor, Guardian One. But be advised that Thallan is also there and listening."

"Uh . . . Lenos, are you all right?"

"Yes, Guardian One. Will you be traveling here for meetings?"

"Lenos, is it true?"

"It's true, Guardian One. I'm in the *Enterprise* and watching the lights of Celerbitan pass below me. I've already spoken with Captain Kirk privately. So has Thallan. Both of us urge you to travel here with a Guardian delegation for conferences. I'm convinced that our future on the Abode is at stake."

"You cannot speak for Thallan. Can he speak for himself?"

"Yes, Guardian One, this is Thallan," the voice of the Technic leader came back. "I confirm everything that Prime Proctor Lenos has just told you. We of the Technic are willing to meet with the Proctorate and the Guardians, because a great change is upon us. There will be no more Ordeals. But we must speak together of this and work out a peaceful solution. Otherwise, I fear there will be conflict, because your prime Guardian Purpose no longer exists to hold Mercan civilization together."

Pallar dropped the communicator to the floor. "I refuse to permit any discussions in which the Technic participates on an equal footing with the ancient and respected Guardians of the Code," he growled. "The Technic was the cause of this, and the Technic must suffer the consequences of overthrowing the established ways of the Code. . . ."

Keeping his eyes on Pallar, Kirk bent down and picked up the communicator. Then he stood up and stared directly up at the Guardian One. "Pallar, I've tried to act with diplomacy and decorum. You've replied time after time with bigoted, biased replies and reactions. I'm willing to forgive those because I understand your background. But since you will not cooperate willingly, I regret to inform you that you have no choice but to meet with us and with the Proctorate and the Technic on the *Enterprise*. Will you choose the three Guardians who will accompany you? Or shall I do it?"

The reaction from Pallar was instinctual. He shouted, "Proctors! Help!"

"Landing force, Plan B," Kirk snapped.

The *Enterprise* landing force moved more quickly than the Mercans because the chosen members of the force had been thoroughly briefed on what to do when that order was given.

Kirk had preselected the Guardian conference group that would accompany him back to the *Enterprise* should Plan B need to be implemented. With his phaser on stun and accompanied by Spock and Sulu, he dropped all the Guardian group save Pallar, Tombah, Noal, and Parna.

As he was doing this, the rest of the landing force formed a precise encompassing grid around the Guardians, phasers at the ready for the Proctors who did indeed show up in the corridors leading to this outside balcony as well as on the parapets above it.

The Proctors got off a few shots. The slugs whistled past, slammed into the floor, and spalled chips and shards before ricocheting off into the darkness. But the Proctors' weapons were charged with black powder; they hadn't progressed to smokeless, flashless gun propellants. As Lenos himself had pointed out, it had been a long time since there'd been any real fighting on Mercan. The flash of the Proctors' guns provided immediate target information to Sulu's security men . . . who didn't miss with their phaser bolts.

"Enterprise, Kirk here. Plan B. Beam us up *now."*

Nothing happened. The communicator had obviously been damaged when Pallar had dropped it.

Spock reacted at once, flipping out his own communicator . . . only to have a stray bullet from a Proctor gun slam it out of his hands. The bullet went through Spock's hand as well.

Even the stoic Spock could not suppress a cry of anguish.

McCoy was at Spock's side immediately. Spock was in obvious pain from the slug that had literally shattered his right hand. But the First Officer didn't fall or faint; he tried to get his hand phaser into his left hand to use it. "Spock, stop that," McCoy snapped at him. "You're wounded and out of action. Shut up and quiet down so that I can get to work on your hand."

It was Sulu who, in the midst of the fire fight, got his communicator out and transmitted the beam-up order.

To the utter amazement of the Proctors who had the group under attack and who were valiantly trying not to hit the Guardians, the twelve from the *Enterprise* and four Guardians dematerialized before their eyes, leaving nothing to shoot at.

Chapter Fourteen

"I'm sorry, Pallar," Kirk apologized as their materialization in the transporter room of the *Enterprise* was completed. "You wouldn't come willingly, so we had to bring you anyway. Whether you know it or not, the entire future of the Abode's at stake . . . and the Guardians were the only group standing in the way of resolving the problem. I'm *not* going to let you stand in the way of getting a stable culture reestablished on the Abode."

Pallar looked around at the strange surroundings. "This is your Keep in the sky?"

"It is. And you're my guests," Kirk told the four Guardians that had been transported up.

"Spock, can you walk to the Sick Bay?" McCoy said as he stepped off the transporter locus with Spock.

Some of the yellowish color had drained from Spock's face. It was obvious he was in severe pain, but his stoic nature wouldn't let him exhibit the agony he felt in his right hand, from which green blood dripped to the transporter locus. "Yes, Doctor, I believe I can. Captain, please carry on without me until Doctor McCoy has repaired the damage of this wound. Then I will join you."

"We'll both join them as soon as *I* say you're fit to do so, Spock. You're *my* patient now," McCoy said as he escorted the First Officer from the transporter room.

Kirk turned back to the Guardians. "Please follow me, Guardians. We have much to show you. . . ."

Pallar shook his head. "You can't keep us here against our will. And I refuse to surrender my traveler control to you, because a Guardian *never* surrenders his traveler control, even to a Proctor. We will all travel out of here back to Celerbitan at once."

Kirk held up his hand. "I wouldn't advise it, Pallar. Do your transporter relays extend their capabilities into the skies? You know that they don't, and so do I." Kirk was frankly bluffing on this one, but he based his bluff on the fact that the Mercans had never considered traveling or transporting off the surface of Mercan. Therefore, he surmised, their transporter system probably couldn't reach out into standard orbit. "Do you want to take the chance of materializing high in the sky over the Abode? If you do, you won't have another chance; you'll die immediately."

"I don't believe you." It was Guardian Tombah.

"You don't have to. I can show you," Kirk replied. "I'll simply advise you not to try it until you have a chance to see for yourself what's involved. If you decide to try, and if we can't rescue you with our traveling device, I'll get another Guardian from the Abode to replace you in the meetings."

Tombah had his traveler control out, but he hesitated before passing his hand over it to activate it. Pallar remarked to him, "James Kirk may be correct, Tombah. Do you wish to risk your life, knowing what happens to one who attempts to use the traveler without full coordinate information? Please, Tombah, I don't wish to lose you."

It was obvious to Kirk that Pallar was slowly beginning to open his mind. One thing for certain: Pallar was as basically intelligent as Prime Proctor Lenos. Leaders don't rise to the top without a considerable amount of intelligence and wisdom, regardless of the culture in which they live.

Kirk stepped down from the transporter platform. "Please follow me, Guardians. You'll not be asked to meet with the Proctorate or the Technic until you've had the chance to see what they've seen and until you've also had the chance to discuss its meaning and implications among yourselves."

As the Guardians followed Kirk, accompanied by Sulu, it was Guardian Tombah who remarked, "This Keep doesn't look like anything that I know the Technic has been able to accomplish."

Stepping into the turbolift, Kirk told him, "I told you we were not of the Technic. And if you'll continue to look and evaluate what you see, you'll understand that this is the abode in which we've come from the Ribbon of Night."

"That remains to be seen," Guardian Parna remarked with some hostility in her voice.

"You'll see it," Sulu added.

They did. The turbolift stopped at Deck 11 in the Dorsal Connector, and the group stepped out into the conference room set up in the former crew lounge.

The reaction of the Guardian group to the view through the ports was totaly different from that of the Technic or the Proctors.

Pallar and Noal went to the ports facing Mercan, while Parna and Tombah stood looking out through the dimmed polarized ports toward Mercaniad. They said nothing for several long minutes while they watched their home planet pass beneath the star ship and the brilliant white disc of Mercaniad march across the sky, finally dipping below the planet's limb. When the Ribbon of Night became visible, Pallar turned to his colleagues and remarked in a quiet voice, "Fellow Guardians, we can no longer refuse to face the facts that are being presented to us. If we persist in our old beliefs, we will go down before the Technic's onslaught upon the old ideas because they now have the new information."

"I agree," Guardian Noal added. "It's very difficult to accept the reality of what we see . . . but we must do so in the face of the possibility of losing our own sanity . . . and whatever control we may have left over the peace and tranquillity of living on the Abode. . . ."

"If I know Prime Proctor Lenos," Tombah put in, "I predict that he's already accepted the new reality. He will not side with us in any conflict with the Technic. . . ."

"But how do we maintain and consolidate our position in the face of this new information?" Parna wanted to know.

"We accept it as an extension of the Code," Pallar tried to explain his jumbled thoughts. He turned to Kirk. "James Kirk, I apologize for our actions."

"No apologies are necessary, Guardian Pallar. It's difficult to accept new information that may not totally agree with what one has previously believed to be true. My people have had to do it many times in their history as we have grown from savagery to the interabode civilization of the United Federation of Planets."

"I'm now very interested in your legend of the United Federation of Planets," Pallar replied. "I'd like to hear more about it."

"Please sit down." Kirk indicated the circle of chairs. "We'll show you what we've shown the Technic and the Proctorate. . . ."

Captain's Log: Stardate 5081.3

All three groups are aboard the ship now, although they're still isolated from one another. We know they're discussing the new situation among themselves. Thallan's asked to beam down to Mercan to talk with the other leaders of the Technic group. I permitted him to go, accompanied by Orun and Sulu. Apparently Prime Proctor Lenos has absolute authority within the Proctorate to make whatever decisions he determines to be best, which is understandable in a paramilitary organization. The Guardian group has not asked to beam down for consultations with their organization. I was probably correct in picking the four Guardians that we beamed up; they're the true leaders and top people in the Guardian organization.

I've asked each of the three groups to indicate to me when they're ready to meet with the other two. I haven't placed a time limit on this. However, if it drags out for more than several days, we'll begin applying pressure to hold the joint meeting. But I'd like to have each group work through their own position, using their own logic and their own intimate knowledge of their position in the Mercan culture.

Spock advises me that this is the best way to proceed. He cites the history of several planets as precedents.

Addendum here: I want this log to include a special commendation for both Lieutenant Commander Spock and Doctor Leonard McCoy, but for separate actions. Spock is to be commended for his bravery and behavior while gravely wounded in the right hand by a Proctor bullet; he was willing to continue to fight even though he was obviously in extreme pain and agony. On the other hand, Doctor McCoy is to be commended for the quick and professional action on his part in coming to Spock's aid under fire and for a marathon session of seven hours in surgery rebuilding Spock's right hand, a feat that required an unusual knowledge of Vulcan-human physiology and an extreme competency in surgery. Spock has been returned to duty, albeit with his right hand covered with plastiskin to accelerate healing.

There's nothing to do now but wait for the Mercans to assimilate the data we presented to them concerning the Federation and the possible options available to them in reorganizing themselves. At the moment, time is not critical. However, should news of the stabilization of Mercaniad manage to leak from the Guardians still on the planet or from the ranks of the Technic, some of whom may have already detected it, we might be faced with a time-critical situation. I sincerely hope this doesn't happen. I'd rather that the reorganization conference here on the *Enterprise* proceed without the pressure of an impending civil war. . . ."

The setting for the joint meeting was different from that for the meetings with the individual groups. Twelve chairs were arranged in a precise circle in the center of the room. Toward the forward end were four more chairs where Kirk, Spock, Scott, and McCoy would sit under the Seal of the United Federation of Planets on the bulkhead. And off to the side was Yeoman Janice Rand's desk and recorder. Kirk had deliberately not included the Federation contingent from the *Enterprise* in the circle of twelve Mercans.

The protocol had been of concern to Kirk. Who should be the first group to arrive? The last? Would the order of entrance imply ranking of a group?

Spock arrived at the most logical solution. There was basically no protocol to govern the situation, only logic, at which the Vulcan was most adept. When Spock had explained his proposal, even McCoy couldn't resist giving him the highest of all compliments, "Logical, Spock. Brilliantly logical."

Spock merely raised his right eyebrow because it *was* an unusual accolade from the ship's doctor.

It was ethnic full-dress Star Fleet uniform for Kirk, Spock, McCoy, and Scott, uniforms that were formal and similar to indicate that this was considered as an extremely high-level conference and with different dress to indicate a unity in diversity among members of the United Federation of Planets. And all four Star Fleet officers would be visibly armed, *not* with the Mercan sidearms, but with the hand phasers that were now recognized by the Mercans to be sidearms highly superior to those of the Abode.

Spock would escort Prime Proctor Lenos. McCoy would escort Guardian One Pallar. And Scott would escort Thallan, of the Technic Peers. Thus escorted, the three Mercans met for the first time aboard the *Enterprise* simultaneously at the turbolift that would carry them to Deck 11.

As anticipated, the atmosphere at the initial greetings at the turbolift were extremely cool but punctiliously correct in the Mercan fashion, even between Pallar and Lenos. But the three Mercans recognized that high protocol was being observed here, something that they now knew was as much a part of the Federation's culture as it was on the Abode. The Mercans knew and understood this protocol, even though it was strange to them.

The escorted leaders were met on Deck 11 by Captain James T. Kirk in full dress uniform. Within seconds, the second turbolift arrived with the remaining three members of each Mercan group, each group accompanied by a single protocol escort from the security division in full dress uniform. However, the protocol escort didn't leave the turbolift, which closed its doors after depositing the Mercan groups.

The meeting had been choreographed as precisely as a classical ballet. The three Mercan groups found themselves seated in a circle facing one another.

But before a single word was uttered, the anthem of the United Federation of Planets blared from audio transducers in the ceiling of the conference room. Simultaneously, Kirk and his officers came to attention and faced the UFP Seal.

It was a show loaded with schmaltz and ceremony . . . and it was deliberate on the part of the Star Fleet officers, who had planned it carefully. The Mercan groups knew right from the start that this conference was theirs, but that there was a higher organization, the UFP, looking over their shoulders. And, following the individual group briefings the Mercans had attended, all of them knew what the UFP was. The Mercans probably didn't understand what the anthem signified, because they'd heard the music only occasionally during the individual briefings, but they certainly understood manners, diplomacy, and protocol because of their armed, polite society.

Whether or not all the Mercans really accepted the reality of the UFP remained to be seen, insofar as Kirk was concerned.

As the music faded, Kirk remained standing. "I welcome the representative groups of Mercan, the Abode of Life, to the United Star Ship *Enterprise* of the Star Fleet of the United Federation of Planets," he began formally. "We are honored to host this conference that is so vitally important in the reorganization of the structure of the civilization of the Abode. We are at your disposal for assistance of any sort. Should you request it, we would be honored to provide a counselor of your choice from among the four of us to act as moderator of your meeting. However, since this meeting concerns the affairs of the Abode, we must decline to act in any manner to lead the conference or otherwise provide active direction of your deliberations. You have grave problems to solve among yourselves . . . and the solutions must be the ones that you arrive at because you and your people on the Abode will be the ones who must henceforth live with those solutions and their consequences. Please feel free to proceed."

The Mercans looked at one another wordlessly for a long minute after Kirk sat down.

Then Pallar stood. "I would speak privately with the people from the Abode," he told Kirk. "It is my understanding that none of you from the United Federation of Planets speak our language yet. If that is the case, would you be kind enough to turn off your language devices. If you do understand our language, I request that the four of you leave the conference room, along with Yeoman Janice Rand, so that we may speak privately."

"We haven't had time to learn your tongue, Pallar. We'll turn off our language translators until you signal us that you wish them turned on again," Kirk replied, reaching down to switch off the Translator hung from a chain around his neck like a pendant. "Gentlemen," he told his officers, "please turn off your Translators."

Pallar immediately sat down, and a polite, soft-spoken conversation began between the twelve Mercans. Kirk was worried. He hadn't anticipated this.

"What's going on, Captain?" Scott wanted to know. "Why would they want to discuss something in private?"

"I don't know," Kirk said with an edginess in his voice. "Yeoman Rand, are the security guards standing by, just in case?"

"Yes, Captain," she replied. "Four of them are in the turbolift at this deck behind the closed doors. I have communication with them."

"Good. Gentlemen, I presume your phasers are on stun, just in case?"

"Captain," Spock put in quietly, "I don't think that this is an illogical act on their part at all. This is the first time that any of these people have had to face one another and talk their way through a solution. I submit to you that their request for privacy is an act of face-saving on their part. They do not wish to let us know of their weakness: inexperience at political and diplomatic bargaining and compromise."

"I agree with Spock's analysis," McCoy added.

"I hope you're right," Kirk told them.

"There is no other logical explanation," Spock reminded him.

"Spock, sometimes things don't proceed logically!" Scott interjected, sounding strangely like Doctor McCoy. "The only things that play by the rules all the time accordin' to logic are engineering devices; they're rational! Haven't you learned that humanoids aren't rational?"

"I have, Mister Scott," Spock replied coolly. "Humans, for example, are not rational beings; they are rationalizing beings."

"I dinna ken whether I've just been insulted or not!" Scott muttered.

"On the other hand, the Mercans are more like humans with a Vulcan background," Spock went on, unperturbed as usual. "Their private discussion is rational."

"I still suspect trouble," Scott admitted.

Pallar suddenly stood up again and, using sign language, requested that the Star Fleet officers turn on their Translators.

"We must apologize for requesting privacy," the Guardian One began. "But we're completely unfamiliar with the protocol and means of conduct of a meeting such as this. The twelve of us therefore request the assistance of the representatives of the United Federation of Planets. Although you refuse to lead us, you've stated that you'll assist and advise. Is this correct?"

Kirk nodded, and since he was not certain that Pallar understood the gesture, added, "You're correct, Guardian One."

"Very well. It would be a great honor and we would be greatly in your debt if you would provide such assistance and advice. The Technic requests that Engineer Montgomery Scott join their group as adviser, while the Proctorate asks Lieutenant Commander Spock to sit with them. The Guardians would request that Doctor McCoy advise and assist us. Together, our three groups from the Abode request that Captain James Kirk preside over this meeting as moderator."

Simultaneously, all twelve Mercans rose, moved

their chairs back to widen the circle, and left a place where the Star Fleet officers could place their chairs.

"This is a very unusual request," Kirk began.

"This is a very unusual meeting," Thallan added.

"And the circumstances are unique," Lenos put in.

"We don't ask you to violate your code of the Prime Directive and General Order Number One," Pallar went on. "You offered assistance. We're requesting it in a way that we jointly believe will help us the most."

This was a totally new slant to the meeting, and it placed it in a completely different perspective insofar as Kirk was concerned. It put him in charge of running the meeting, a position that he'd attempted to avoid. And it put his officers in the difficult position of having to advise the Mercan groups. It was *not* the way Kirk would have wanted to see the meeting proceed. He saw himself in the conquistador role again, and he didn't like it.

On the other hand, the Mercans themselves had requested it after private consultations among themselves. No wonder Pallar had asked for privacy in discussing it; the Guardian One had been afraid that the other groups might not agree, and this would have been viewed by the Mercans as an insult to the officers of the *Enterprise*.

But *why* had they jointly agreed to it so quickly, for it had taken them less than five minutes? And why was the meeting progressing so smoothly right from the start? Why weren't there more objections from various factions? Why wasn't there any obvious argument? And why had the Mercans agreed to—and in fact insisted that—the officers of the *Enterprise* assume such an active role in the discussions?

"I'll agree to act as moderator of the meeting, which is a position in which I won't be forced to impose my cultural biases on the rest of you," Kirk replied with caution. "However, I can't speak for my officers. It's up to each of them to individually agree to advise and assist the Mercan groups as you've requested. But before I ask them, please answer a question for me . . . and don't be afraid to speak truthfully, because I won't take offense at the truthful answer. *Why* have you requested us to step in to advise and assist you in the reestablishment of your cultural organization when you know that we believe you must do the job yourselves?"

Pallar spoke first. "We of the Guardians have never had to do this before. We don't know how to do it. We've discussed matters with the Proctorate before, but we've always been the ones who have given the final directives, even though those directives may have been based on the recommendations of the Proctorate."

"We don't know where to begin," Prime Proctor Lenos went on. "We're like children who have just become learning-old."

"We never expected that the awesome responsibility of having to reorganize our civilization would ever fall upon our shoulders," Thallan added. "In the Technic, we were interested only in arriving at the truth about ourselves and the Universe. We had no anticipation that our role would grow to the point where we'd be called upon to actually run the Abode."

"But why the sudden agreement to cooperate?" Kirk wondered aloud.

"Didn't you want that when you established this meeting and went through the protocol as you did?" Pallar asked in return.

"Of course. But I didn't think that you'd agree to agree this quickly," Kirk admitted.

Thallan smiled the broad, toothy grin of a Mercan. "Ah, just as we once underestimated you, now you have underestimated us, James Kirk."

"This is the only rational approach toward solving the problems," Lenos pointed out. "The other approach is to fight . . . and we haven't fought for a long time. And I really don't want to fight, as we once discussed, James Kirk."

"And since it's the only rational approach, did you believe that we would be any less rational than you humans and Vulcans, once presented with irrefutable data?" Pallar admitted. He looked at Scott, Spock, and McCoy. "Come, join us, we have much work to do. It will not be easy. We will not always agree with one another in the process of establishing the solution. But we need and want *your* help because you have, in your own cultures, solved some of the problems we face. We may not adopt your solutions, but we want to know how and why you arrived at the ones you did."

"It will be an honor to help you work toward a logical solution," Spock told them.

"I'll also consider it a personal honor and a deep responsibility to advise you as best I can," McCoy agreed.

"I'll also consider it a high honor to participate with the Technic group," Scott put in.

Under the circumstances, Kirk was very glad that Janice Rand had her tricorder running to make a record of these proceedings. He was once again concerned over General Order Number One, but the record would show that the people of the *Enterprise* were *asked* to step in and help. They took their positions in the circle.

Then there was dead silence while the Mercans simply looked at Kirk.

"Citizens of Mercan, begin," the Captain of the *Enterprise* remarked uneasily.

"Where?" Pallar asked.

"How do we start?" Thallan asked.

"What should be discussed first?" Lenos wanted to know.

It was Kirk who didn't answer immediately.

How *do* you write the Constitution for Utopia?

He recalled the Star Fleet Academy class in xenosociology in which they'd tried to do just that, and it started out the same way: where do you begin?

At the beginning, of course, he realized.

"The Guardians and the Proctorate didn't always exist on the Abode," Kirk pointed out. "Go back into your legends and stories. Tell us what happened and how the civilization of the Abode was established as it was when we arrived. *Then,* we'll go on from there. Correction: *you* will go on from there, because then you'll know how to start and in which direction to go."

Chapter Fifteen

Captain's Log: Stardate 5099.5

It seems incredible that we've done it in *ten short days*. It took fifty-five delegates one hundred and twenty-two days to draft the Constitution of the United States of America in 1787 . . . and even then it was an imperfect document that required continual alteration for centuries thereafter. And it took over a hundred people, accompanied by staffs totaling more than a thousand assistants, nearly two years to draft the Articles of Federation of the UFP on Babel. More years of work were needed to come up with the statutes for the Interplanetary Court of Justice and those regulating interplanetary commerce.

But the twelve Mercans, assisted by four officers of Star Fleet Command, one yeoman, and the library computer of the USS *Enterprise,* have, in ten days, drafted what the Mercans proudly call the Enterprise Agreement.

How good is it? How long will it last? I wish I knew.

Unlike those who drafted the Constitution of the USA, we had the knowledge of the known universe available instantaneously at our fingertips in the ship's computer memory banks. Unlike the delegates to the Babel Convention, there was only one planet with three power groups involved.

Maybe this wasn't a hasty agreement after all. Maybe it will work. But the Mercans are going to have to find out for themselves because they're the ones who wrote the Enterprise Agreement, and they're the ones who agreed to abide by it. Scott, Spock, McCoy, and I acted only as advisers, providing the inputs the Mercans wanted from the history of the planets of the Federation.

The Agreement isn't simple. After all, the Mercan culture isn't simple. In our short stay here, we haven't even started to unravel it, much less experience a great deal of it. For example, the Mercans possess highly developed entertainment arts, both passive and performing. They have an educational system, but we haven't had the chance to see it because we've been too busy; it must be a good system, because it trains their citizens well in a complex planet-wide culture tied together by the cheap and instantly available traveler system. Mercan is something like Earth might have been if travel had turned out to be as universal as communications there.

The crux of the matter was going back to the roots of the system that had existed when we arrived here. I'll leave a lot of the analysis up to the Federation xeno-sociology and anthropology teams who will follow. But it's very simple and goes right back to the basic definition of a social organization, something we knew about on Earth for centuries but which was turned into a science when the first space colonies provided a means to test social systems in isolation. In any social organization, an individual relinquishes some basic rights in order to participate in the greater security of the group.

This requires some modification of individual behavior, plus some means to coerce an unwilling individual into the proper mode of behavior. This requires laws, rules, regulations, and codes of behavior. I live under several every day and don't even bother to think about them. The Mercans have lived under similar conditions for as long as they can remember.

When the Mercans realized that the end of the Ordeal would not require a complete change of social organization, but a *modification* of what already existed, it was relatively simple, according to my First Officer, Mister Spock, who has already analyzed the outcome to his logical satisfaction.

Once the Ordeal was no longer a factor in Mercan life, none of the three groups was either a challenge or a threat to the other.

The Guardians were just that: the guardians of the laws of Mercan. It was unfortunate that their remote ancestors, being the intelligentsia of the planet at the time, also discovered the Mysteries of Mercaniad that permitted them to predict the Ordeal. That grew out of proportion with respect to the real role of the Guardians; they are the ones who enact and interpret the rules of conduct between Mercans and their various institutions. Once the Guardians understood that, *they* became the *de facto* government of the Abode . . . as they really were all along. And under the provisions of the Agreement, they'll attempt to expand their ranks. They think they can do it by means of competitive examination once they've learned how our lawyers are trained and then admitted to the legal practice by examination. Well, we'll have to see how it works for the Mercans. . . .

The Proctorate, on the other hand, is the Mercan equivalent of the social organization that enforces the rules of social conduct. Elsewhere, they

may be called the police, the military, the guard, or
Star Fleet. There was not much need to change the
Proctorate under the Enterprise Agreement because they already have their own procedure for
selecting, training, and admitting new members. I
have no reservations about the possibility of the
Proctors taking over; in the first place, as Lenos
admitted, they haven't fought in a long time because the *code duello* takes care of most of the
fighting urge of the Mercans of *both* sexes. (I don't
think I mentioned the fact that the Mercan women,
including Delin, carry sidearms as well, and that
the Mercans protect their women but have no
chivalrous code that we humans inherited from the
Arabs.) I know why Lenos and his Proctors chose
Spock to sit with them; like the Proctors, Spock is
basically a very violent man who keeps his emotions under tight control and who doesn't like to
fight . . . except during *pon farr*, when I personally
know that Spock can be very violent indeed. And
to some extent, I too understand the Proctors. The
military/naval profession is a strange one because
of the reluctance of its professional members to
engage in the activities of the profession.

The Technic, who thought they were the political
saviors of the Abode, discovered when the chips
were down they really didn't want the job because
they were interested in things, not people. This
isn't true of all the Technic members, because
those who were the staunchest anti-Guardian Technics would probably have made better Guardians,
even though they were rebels. The Technic was
afraid of the Guardians who were afraid of the
Technic. After all, the Technic was discovering
things that didn't match the dogma of the Guardians; the Guardians were afraid that the Technic
knowledge would unseat them as "keepers of the
faith," so they tried to suppress the Technic. They
were a threat to each other. In stabilizing Mercan-

iad and removing the Ordeal as a factor in Mercan life, we didn't realize at that time we were removing that threat. The Technic knows now that they're free to investigate anything they want to, but they also now realize that this freedom of inquiry carries with it the obligation to openly disseminate what they learn, especially to the Guardians, who, in turn, now realize that they must modify the rules and codes on the basis of new information from the Technic.

I think it's stable. But I'm not sure. The Enterprise Agreement includes checks and balances, and one of the most important of these is the willingness of the Mercans to accept the Articles of Federation of the UFP.

Now, at last, we can get busy putting the *Enterprise* into shape to return to the Orion Arm. But the best that I can do is look over Scott's shoulder and try to smooth out diplomatic problems that occur. . . .

"Captain, it isn't goin' to work. I canna get these Technic people to follow my instructions. They keep comin' up with their own little improvements," the Engineering Officer complained to Kirk. "I give 'em the worn part . . . and they give me back three *exactly* like it: worn out, even to the scratch and rub marks!"

"Well, what did you tell them, Scotty?" Kirk wanted to know.

"I told 'em to make me a new part just like the old one."

"And they did, didn't they?"

"I'll say they did!"

"Why don't you give them a drawing instead?"

"Because their dimensional system is different and their number system is a mess, as I told ye before. Also, their alloying techniques are different."

"Have you tried showing them the warp drive and

explaining it to them? Wouldn't that help them understand what you want from them?"

"I did that, Captain," Scotty kept complaining. "Othol understands it perfectly, he says. And he keeps wantin' to make *improvements* in *my* engines."

"Well, they've taken a different cut at antimatter power. Will some of the improvements work?"

"I canna tell until we try to exceed Warp Factor One. And if the improvement doesn't work right, it's a kind of final way to do testing. I don't think you could call it 'nondestructive testing' under any set of rules."

Kirk knew that this was just his engineer's way of discharging tension, although he didn't dismiss it entirely from his mind. They were still a long way from a Starbase, and the *Enterprise* had to be able to sustain Warp Factor Six once under way.

But Kirk was breathing a lot easier. The remaining problems were mainly technical in nature; they could be solved, given enough time. And with the Enterprise Agreement, time was no longer as critical as it had been.

As a matter of fact, it gave Kirk the opportunity to give his crew a little of the "rest and relaxation" that their original scientific survey mission had been intended to provide. It would serve another purpose as well, because the Abode would be petitioning for membership in the Federation . . . and a shore leave by thoroughly briefed Star Fleet personnel would provide an interesting two-way street of information and understanding.

Since *Enterprise* personnel on the Abode would be subject to the Code, the obvious person to brief them on it was Lenos, Prime Proctor of Mercan. Lenos only had to do it once. Kirk assigned Uhura to make a briefing tape to be shown to all personnel before beaming down. This tape not only provided the necessary information on the ultrapolite Mercan culture for the *Enterprise* crew members—some of whom were from some planetary cultures that were rather loose

and frank in comparison—but also gave Kirk a valuable
documentary to take back.

Naturally, there were confrontations, as there always
are when two greatly different cultures interface. But
Kirk's standing order was to wear hand phasers in sight,
set to stun, there being severe penalties for those crew
members who fired a phaser on Mercan with any other
setting. In spite of the crudity of the Mercan hand
weapons, some of the Mercans turned out to be
reasonably good marksmen. Bones McCoy had to
patch a few holes in some of the crew members and
remove steel slugs from others, including the scrutable
Mister Sulu, who was not the samurai he thought
himself to be. . . .

But Sulu turned up with a magnificent collection of
Mercan hand weapons for which he traded part of his
collection of Earth swords. *Somehow* he managed to
get several members of Scotty's harried engineering
crew to fit out a crude shooting range down in the
secondary hull. Kirk didn't discover this until much
later, although Sulu regaled his Captain with the glories
of collecting Mercan firearms.

Several weeks passed. The repairs to the warp drive
were indeed extensive and were not ameliorated by the
difficulties of matching Star Fleet technology with
Mercan technology.

"I'm taking aboard a large quantity of these low-
grade Mercan dilithium crystals, Captain. We've made
up a unit that uses several of them in parallel, and we
can operate them as standby units. I dinna want to trust
this long trip to dilithiums whose condition may have
been strained by the gravitational jump that brought us
here."

"When can we plan to get under way, Scotty?" Kirk
wanted to know. Things seemed to be working out well
on Mercan, and Kirk wanted to get moving again. The
sooner they got back to Starbase 4 and the sooner
the Federation was able to send a ship back to Mercan,
the better. The Enterprise Agreement might be work-

ing now, but only Kirk knew how fragile it might become if the Federation did not respond with its presence in short order.

Scott held up four fingers of his right hand. "Four days . . . if I can make this bloody Mercan technology match with ours. We've got a lot of testing to do. . . ."

"Then everything's been basically repaired?"

"Aye, but I dinna ken it will work, Captain."

"Mister Scott, we will break orbit in six watches and proceed under impulse power so you can make your tests in an under-way situation," Kirk instructed him.

"Captain, if something blows, we're in trouble."

"It won't blow, Scotty. You're too good an engineer to let that happen."

Any chance of engine trouble, Kirk knew, was possible but remote. It would be a concern until the ship passed Warp Factor One, but Kirk was willing to risk it.

He was far more concerned about the course home. If they encountered any of the extreme gravitational turbulence that had brought them to the Abode in the first place, it could mean real trouble with a hay-wired warp drive unit . . . which is what Kirk considered it to be until Scott had the chance to go over it very thoroughly with the sophisticated equipment of Starbase 4. He put Spock, Sulu, and Chekov to work on the problem of getting back to the Orion Arm in the safest and most expeditious fashion.

"I see no problem, Captain," Spock remarked in an offhand manner. "Having once been through such a gravitational fold, I'm aware of the sensor indications that precede the event. As a result, I can assure you that I will be most vigilant indeed to ensure that it doesn't happen again."

"I know that, Spock. But let's make sure."

The departure from Mercan was, as Kirk expected and wanted it to be, formal in the best sense of Mercan politeness. The first ceremony took place in the atrium of the Guardian Villa overlooking the wine-dark sea around Celerbitan. Gifts were exchanged first, Kirk presenting Pallar with a tricorder in reciprocation for an elaborately decorated traveler control from Pallar. That control unit would be of great interest to Federation technical people, and Kirk knew that the Technic would pore over the tricorder, giving Mercan its first communications/information technology other than the computers of its traveler, commercial, and educational systems. There were no flags, no anthems, no twenty-one-gun salutes; those were not a part of Mercan protocol. But it was different during the second and final ceremony in the recreational garden on Deck 8 in the *Enterprise,* where Kirk, Spock, McCoy, and Scotty beamed up with the Mercans. There was an honor guard, the UFP banner, and an anthem. Such things would be part of the diplomatic scene at UFP Headquarters, and Kirk had no real choice but to carry on the tradition here, in spite of its wide divergence from that of Mercan.

Kirk was not surprised when Pallar, Lenos, and Thallan—representing the three major organizations of Mercan—presented the two ambassadors *pro tem* from Mercan to the Federation: Delin and Orun.

"I know you first met these two as young rebels with the Technic," Pallar explained, "but, as you understand now, they would have been outstanding Guardians except for their excessive curiosity. Under the Enterprise Agreement, it no longer makes a difference. I believe they're open-minded and intelligent enough to properly represent the Abode to the Federation . . . and I rather envy the things they're going to see and learn about."

"We'll have stories to tell when we return," Delin promised.

"And this time I think you'll all believe them," Orun added.

Once the three Mercan leaders had beamed back down, Kirk reverted to his role of star-ship captain with great relief. But he did remember his diplomatic role

enough to ask, "Delin, would you and Orun wish to
watch our departure from the Bridge?"

He didn't need to ask.

In the command seat again, Kirk *knew* they were
going home in spite of the strange and sometimes
baffling repairs that Scotty had made with Mercan help.
Kirk knew his ship. He knew she was ready for star
travel. He looked around the Bridge with satisfaction.
"Departments report, please."

Chekov did not look up. "Course plotted and laid
in."

Sulu did turn and flash a brief smile at Kirk. "Ready
to leave orbit, sir."

Kirk punched a button on the arm of the seat.
"Mister Scott, how about it?"

"As ready as we'll ever be, Captain."

Kirk turned to face Uhura, who was sitting impassively at her console. "I'm afraid we haven't kept you
very busy on this mission, Lieutenant," he remarked.

"That's quite all right, Captain. I've enjoyed the
rest," Uhura replied with a smile.

"Well, we'll get you busy again. Put Mercan on the
main screen and keep it there as we leave orbit."

"Aye, sir."

Spock was sitting passively with his fingertips together forming a steeple. "Sir, the ship is ready in all
respects for star flight."

"Thank you, Mister Spock. Mister Sulu, impulse
power. Take us out of orbit. Accelerate to Warp Factor
Point-nine-five and report reaching."

"All ahead on impulse power. We have left orbit."

It was slow at first, but the image of Mercan could be
seen getting smaller as the *Enterprise* moved gradually
away from the planet under impulse drive.

"You have a beautiful Abode," Kirk told the two
young diplomats. "I'm sure that it'll be a most welcome
member to the Federation."

Orun's voice was a bit unsteady, and Kirk noticed a
tear in the corner of Delin's eye. "It's not at all like

using the traveler for the first time; it is more like becoming responsible-old and leaving home to make a new home."

Delin merely rubbed her eye and added, "Well, Orun, is it anything like you imagined it to be in that argument that led to your confrontation with Othol . . . and that was interrupted by the arrival of Captain Kirk?"

The young Mercan looked at his companion. "No, it's not. And please do not remind me of that again, because I missed widely. . . ."

"I'm glad that you did," Delin admitted.

The turbolift door swished open and Bones McCoy walked in, making his usual post-departure visit to the Bridge, a ritual that he rarely missed unless there was serious work to be done in Sick Bay. He stepped to the side of the command seat and watched the image of Mercan grow smaller on the viewscreen. "Congratulations, Jim. It's not every star-ship captain who manages to bring a whole new civilization into the Federation."

"Bones, it wasn't easy."

"Knowing you, I never had the slightest doubt you'd manage to bring it off."

"I did."

"I know you did. I'm responsible for periodically reviewing the captain's log."

Kirk nodded as he watched Mercan grow smaller on the screen. "Bones, in some ways, I still feel like Hernando Cortes or Francisco Pizarro. . . ."

"Really? It seems to me that there were other ship captains who discovered new civilizations and managed to arrange for the amalgamation of those cultures into the mainstream," McCoy observed quietly. "Have you ever considered comparing yourself to Commodore Matthew C. Perry instead?"

Spock left his post at the library computer console and walked over to stand on the other side of the command seat from McCoy. "If it will make you feel any better, Captain, Mercan had a very high probability of being discovered by the Federation, since it lies directly in the path of the Federation's exploration and colonization efforts into the Sagittarius Arm. Our own discovery of Mercan falls well within the three-sigma limit of the probability of its discovery in this century. . . ."

"And I suppose that bit of statistical gobbledygook also falls within the same three-sigma limit you quoted when you wanted to tickle Mercaniad, Spock," McCoy interjected acidly.

"Doctor, I'm surprised that you don't use more statistical evaluation in your medical work. Although I am appreciative of your efforts in rebuilding my right hand, I must say I was appalled when you were not able to give me any probabilities concerning whether or not I would ever be able to use it again. . . ."

"Spock, I don't run my Sick Bay that way. When I do a surgical-reconstruction job such as your hand, I *know* it's going to be all right. I don't need any statistical analysis to tell me whether or not I'm doing *my* job. . . . Of course, *your* job may be different. . . ."

"Gentlemen . . . gentlemen!" Kirk remonstrated. "Let me add that it's obvious neither of you learned anything about tactful mannerisms from the Mercan culture."

"On the contrary, Captain," Spock replied. "I found the Mercan culture to be highly logical. As Doctor McCoy himself pointed out, the Mercans are similar to Vulcans, especially in the realm of logical thought processes. And I might add, Captain, that you handled the entire situation on Mercan quite logically."

"Thank you for the compliment, Mister Spock."

"There is no logical reason to thank me, Captain."

"Spock, there you go again!" McCoy burst out in frustration. "Can't you accept plain and simple gratitude?"

"Doctor," Spock said slowly, "gratitude is an emotion signifying resentment, another irrational emotion."

"Captain, we're approaching Warp Factor Point-nine-five. Standing by the warp drive," Sulu announced from the helm.

Kirk pushed the intercom button for Engineering. "Scotty, how did the tests come out?"

"I think she'll work, Captain."

"Are you positive, Scotty?"

There was a brief silence. "Aye, Captain. I've done my best on her. She's ready."

"Forward view on the main screen," Kirk snapped.

"Forward view," Uhura replied. The screen showed no stars, only the band of the Orion Arm ahead.

"Helmsman, accelerate to Warp Factor Two."

"Coming to Warp Factor Two."

There was just the briefest shudder in the *Enterprise*. The band of light that was the galactic arm spread in the middle, widened into the star bow of relativistic velocities, then blinked into nothingness, to be quickly replaced by the computer-generated scene as reconstructed from subspace stellar emissions.

"Engineering, report."

"She's running beautifully, Captain," was Scotty's obviously delighted reply.

"Mister Sulu, accelerate to Warp Factor Six." Kirk rose from his command seat.

"We're going home," he said quietly, as much to his ship as to his crew.